Trying for You

LEYA LAYNE

Trigger Warnings

While this book is meant to be a cozy romance with spice, there are discussions of topics that could be triggering for readers. To be respectful to those who need warnings and those who see them as spoilers, I have placed the trigger warnings on my website. Scan this code to check the site.

Trying for You was originally published in part within Heating Up in Cole County: A Cozy Romance Anthology in 2025 as Try Me.

TRYING FOR YOU

COLE COUNTY MEMORIES

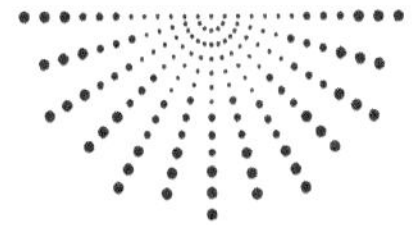

LEYA LAYNE

"When the body and mind align, the heart's not far behind."

DON'T GET MY HOPES UP

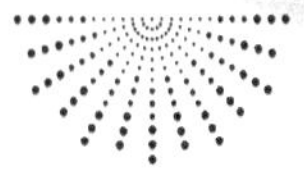

Joanna

The bell on the front door barely rings when Taylor's voice echoes through the empty store into the stockroom where I'm pulling out additional shovels. The other week's unexpected snowstorm had lots of new residents in here buying winter prep materials. We'll likely need to place an additional order to ensure there are enough to make it through the entire season if this is how we're starting. Of course, there are worse problems to have.

"JD! Where in the hell are ya?"

For some reason, she's taken to calling me JD. Apparently, Joanna has too many syllables. She calls her best friend J rather than her two-syllable name—Jordan—so now I'm JD like the name of our hardware store.

"Back here with the shovels. What's gotten into you?" I mumble a quick 'besides my dad' and giggle to myself. I've barely fixed my face when she busts into the aisle.

"Girl, I have some news you're going to want to hear!"

"Please don't tell me you're pregnant," I say with as much

stoicism as I can muster when laughter threatens to burst out of me.

"Fuck off! You and Jacob will be the only ones calling me mom!"

We both laugh at that. The two of us have grown close over the past ten months and have begun bantering like sisters. Though she seems to have the closer-knit, emotion-sharing relationship with Morgan, my best friend from childhood, we are the fun sisters. Having her around has helped with the loss I'd been feeling at my twin, Jacob, spending all his free time at Gretna House. Ugh, I still hate that Morgan named her BnB after that miserable woman. Her grandmother, Gretna Humphries, was a real bitch.

"So, what's the big news?"

"The rodeo is coming to town at the beginning of April."

With the shovel handles in one hand, I put my other hand on my hip and look at her with pursed lips. "That's not news, T. The rodeo comes every April."

"You didn't let me finish. I know someone whose team is coming, and they have an opening for a hand to help with the horses." She waggles her brows at me, and my pulse jumps.

"A hand?"

"Yeah, they have a few women on their team already, so they're not intimidated by strong women who know their shit and can do what the big, strong cowboys do." She lifts her arms to show flexed biceps, moving them up and down in a mockery of muscled men.

I laugh at her antics and then walk by, passing off a couple of the shovels into her hands. Might as well take advantage of her being here bothering me on her day off.

"What's that got to do with me?" I ask, trying to keep the excitement at bay to not get my feeling hurt by the letdown.

"What's that got to...what the hell do you think that's got to do with you? Did you not tell me that you were interested in maybe joining a rodeo team and traveling the circuit with them?"

"I mean, yes, that is..." I trail off while I place the shovels in their new display at the front of the store before turning back to face her. "That is the dream. I mean, just because they're looking for someone doesn't mean they'll choose me."

The look she gives me is one of confusion. Shit, I don't want to tell her I'm scared of rejection. I want this, but the choices I've made in life weren't simply to make my family happy. I've taken the easy way out.

"Cut to the chase, Taylor, and don't get my hopes up."

"I've already talked to my friend. My friend who happens to be Jordan's older brother. Jordan's older brother who I've known nearly my entire life. I told him that you're strong, motivated, and can work independently and as part of a team to get things done."

I smile at her description of me. Taylor has a way of seeing the good in people even if they can't see it themselves. Her next words create a lump in my throat and have tears pricking the backs of my eyes.

"He put in a good word for you at my request, and they're willing to take you on as a trial run from January until the rodeo gets here to Cole County in April. At that point, you will either have decided that scene is not really for you or that the team is not a good fit. Either that, or you'll love it, and they'll love you enough that you'll keep going to the next stop."

"You're serious? It's a done deal, sight unseen?"

MY FEELINGS MATTER

*J*oanna

The holidays pass in a blur. Every day brings me one step closer to leaving for Double D Ranch. Every hour that passes makes my heartbeat quicken. And every minute deepens the pit in my stomach because I haven't yet told Pa or Jake about the offer or that I've accepted it. I'm sure Jake will be fine with it, even happy for me, but Pa freaked when he heard I was even thinking about leaving Colliers Town.

That day plays over and over in my mind. Not only because Taylor got hurt here at the store, but because it was the first time I'd seen disappointment in my father's eyes. Hurt and disappointment at me.

"When were you going to tell me that you planned to join the fucking circus?"

His voice bellowed through the storeroom. He rarely yelled, and I can't remember the last time he'd been upset enough with me to yell. I've always been the level-headed one, the child who does all the right things and takes care of everything and everyone. I'm the one who got married, planned to settle down and have children. I'm the one who took over the family business. Hell, I'm the one who took care of him when our entire world fell apart.

"Good morning to you too, Pa."

That morning, the sarcastic retort was the only thing I could muster as I tried to make sense of his anger.

"I had to hear that shit from your brother? I told him he was full of shit, that you wouldn't even consider such a thing."

Though he's always been a bit of a grump, the hurt and anger in his tone was hard to take in, but it was nothing compared to the pain I felt when he lowered his voice.

"You're not, right?"

All I could do was stare at him from behind the computer monitors. I watched his eyes take in the state of my desk, papers strewn across the top. I saw the moment guilt crept in at the paper ledgers I was steadily entering into my spreadsheets on the computer. Pa hates the computer and can't understand why I choose to keep the books on it. In this way, he's a relic, but I never want him feeling bad about all the help he gives Taylor and me when I'm not around. That day, I was still catching up from when I'd been out sick with the flu a few weeks prior.

"I'm not joining the circus, old man. I'm not a fucking clown, and I'm too damn old to swing from a trapeze."

His step back had me feeling guilty. Though I've blessed Jake up one side and down the other many times, I'd never cussed at Pa before that day. I apologized, of course, but it didn't change the reality of what I was planning.

"So, it's not a joke? You're thinking of leaving."

The resigned tone in his voice told me it was far past time that he and I sat down for a heart-to-heart. Though I remember initially suggesting the loveseat as a way to get the computer monitors from between us, other memories flood in, and I move from my desk to the loveseat with a crooked smile. Pa had put the loveseat in the office for Ma, so she could have somewhere comfortable to sit when she'd come in to help with the store. She was much better with people than him, so Jacob and I often played on the rug as small children while he hid here in the back running the numbers. Every one of us has taken a nap on this loveseat at one time or another. My neck hurts thinking about how uncomfortable it is to twist myself into the small space as I've grown taller. With a heavy heart full of memories, I lay down and stretch my legs over the arm. It was that day here in the office that I realized there was something brewing between Taylor and my pa, even if they hadn't acknowledged it themselves yet. She'd interrupted the tension between us by popping her head through the storeroom door.

"Is everything ok?" her unsure voice came from the open doorway.

"We're fine," I responded.

Pa looked back and forth between Taylor and me before he asked her to excuse us in the softest voice I've heard him use with her since she started working here. I nodded in agreement, and she slowly closed the door behind her before I grabbed Pa's hands to keep them from clenching into fists.

"I had planned to talk to you this evening after I closed the shop," I said, breaking the silence. "I'm guessing big mouth assumed I already had. I'm sorry for that. You should have heard it from me first."

A single tear slipped down his cheek, and it nearly broke me.

"Pa, look at me, please."

He shook his head, unwilling to let me see his eyes. A lump formed in my throat, but I couldn't go back.

"Pa, I need you to let me explain. I need you to listen. Afterwards, you can feel however you need to, but I need you to hear me."

He took a deep breath and eventually choked out a sad sounding "Why?"

"Because I'm your daughter, and I need to know that my feelings matter to you too." Sadness seeped into my voice, though I'd wanted to remain resolute.

When he finally lifted his eyes to mine, blinking away the tears evident in the rim, I gave him my most earnest smile. With another deep breath, he gestured for me to continue.

"You and Jacob are the most important people in my life. For the longest time, you two being okay was the only thing that mattered to me." My smile faltered, though he nodded in agreement. "Putting all my thoughts, energy, and emotions into you both..." I paused to take my own shuddering deep breath. "Well, it left nothing for me. I forgot that I mattered too."

He scoffed, and bitterness rose in my throat before his words reminded me that none of this was done to cause intentional harm. "Of course you mattered. You've always mattered to me and your brother. We need you!" He said the last words with vehemence, and a tear fell from my eye.

"That's the thing, Pa. You need me, but what about what I need?"

He stared at me as if seeing me for the first time. So many emotions played across his face that I could hardly keep up. "My God, JoJo." He released my hands and shrunk into himself, turning away from me. "Have I really been that selfish all these years?" I grabbed his hands again, willing him to look at me, holding steady until he did. "Your ma would be so proud of you," he said, voice choked with emotion. "Not only have you managed to keep this store running successfully, but you also kept our family from shattering, and you got this old man to admit his shortcomings. I'm so sorry, JoJo."

With a shake of my head, I dismissed his apology. "I did what I felt was right. I took care of you because you needed it and because I was afraid to let anything else in our lives change. I don't think I could have handled any more change. I needed this store to keep me grounded. I couldn't lose you, and you were slipping away. And Jacob was never fully himself since returning from bootcamp. It was too much to take in, and I'm too much of a fighter to have let it all go."

After a moment of silence, he chuckled, and I took my first full breath since the conversation began. "You most definitely are a scrappy one. I couldn't be prouder of the woman you are."

"But now, things are good, better than good. Jacob and Morgan have reunited. You've returned to us whole, or at least more like yourself every day. In fact, you're almost better than ever with all the jokes and smiles these past couple months."

"Was I really that miserable of an old man?"

"Not to me, old man, but yeah, you were a mean SOB sometimes."

His exaggerated gesture of putting a hand over his heart and dramatic 'Ouch!' had me laughing aloud. "Now, it's time for me to find me. I can't do that here."

He let out a sigh. "How long have you been thinking about this?"

"Almost as long as Taylor's been here. It seemed like a light broke through the clouds when she arrived."

"And she knows about your plans to leave? Will she continue to work here?"

"Yeah, Pa. She's been my confidante and sounding board since day one. In fact, she's the reason I was finally able to see my own happiness as important enough to take this step."

His eyes narrowed, brows creasing. "Are you telling me that pixie girl is responsible for this change in you?"

I put my hand on his arm, knowing I needed to nip this line of thinking in the bud. "Now, Pa, don't you turn that around into something bad. I needed someone to talk to who wasn't benefiting from me holding myself back. Morgan was too busy getting all lovey-dovey with Jake in their renewed relationship, or she would've been the one I confided in. Taylor saw my pain, my confusion, my sadness and asked about it. So don't you go blaming her. I'm grateful for her. And that's why I'm asking her to stay on as your assistant while I'm gone. She can keep an eye on you too."

"I don't need a damn babysitter!" He jumped up from the loveseat and stood looking down at me. "I ran this store since you were in elementary school."

"With mom's help!" I yelled back. "You didn't do that shit alone. You may be less of a grump now, at least most of the time, but that doesn't mean you can manage it all yourself. She knows the store, the items, the ordering, the inventory, and she's learning the people." I ignored his glare and pushed through. "Besides, knowing you're not alone here, doing the work of two or three people, will help me feel less guilty about leaving."

A smile crosses my lips as I think about the subtle acknowledgment of the truth in my statement. I like to think he would have eventually come around to accept my plan, but we never got a chance to finish the conversation when everything crashed in the other room. The next couple weeks had everyone focused on Taylor and her recovery, physically and mentally. Her stepfather showing up at the hospital, and Pa kicking his ass, really put a damper on whatever plans any of us had. Now, so much time has gone by that I've been afraid to bring it back up. With less than two weeks to go before my departure, however, I can't keep putting it off.

3

CLENCHED TEETH AND PROMISES

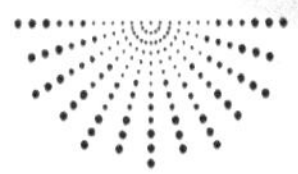

Junior

"Dude, Jerry just got kicked in the leg by Clementine."

I look up from my paperwork where I've been checking farrier and groomer schedules, deciding who's going on the road with us and who's staying. Though it's nice to be back at the ranch when we can swing it during rodeo season, it's like the work has piled up just waiting for me. And now this.

"What do you mean? Clementine isn't a kicker."

"Not usually, but he was brushing her hind leg, and she clipped him."

"Fuck! Get the vet out here to check her leg. He had to have hit a sore spot for her to lash out. We need her on the circuit, and we leave in just a few weeks."

"What about Jerry?"

"What about him?" I say, my patience waning as I look at the papers strewn across my desk.

"He's gonna be laid up for a minute."

"Shit! So, she got him good?" I don't have time for this. We're already short-staffed due to the holidays.

"Shannon doesn't think he broke anything, but his leg's swollen already, so I had Travis take him for an X-ray."

"Ok, thanks, Kells. Keep me posted. I'm gonna try and get some of this paperwork taken care of. If y'all need me out in the barn, let me know."

She nods and starts toward the door before she turns back around. "When's the new hand start? She staying or going?"

I close my eyes and sigh. I hadn't thought about that woman again since I told Taylor we'd hire her on for a trial run. We were in the thick of back-to-back showcases at the time. Bringing her on means I definitely have to go home and bring her back with me or have her come earlier than planned, so she'll be ready when we go back out. Fuck! With one of my guys out of commission, I don't have time to go home.

"We agreed she'd join us on the first, so next week. She's from a town real close to my hometown, so I was going to go home for New Year's and see my folks then bring Joanna back with me."

Kelly Anderson, my barn manager, eyes me curiously. "This Joanna doesn't drive?"

I chuckle. "I'm assuming she does. I simply meant I'd introduce myself and make sure she made it here, whether she drives herself or rides is up to her."

"Do you know this woman?"

I clench my teeth. This was the question I didn't want to answer for anyone. I hired her on a trial basis as a favor to Taylor. Just like my sister, Jordan, Taylor can damn near talk me into anything. When she told me how well everyone there in Colliers Town has treated her after she left home, I felt like giving the woman a chance was a way of paying back the kindness.

"Not directly, no. But I have it on good authority that she's a strong worker, intelligent, knows horses, and is good people."

Kelly seems to accept that answer and closes the door behind her. I'm going to be mucking stalls for a month out of guilt if Joanna doesn't live up to the hype I just gave her. Who cares that

I'm the owners' right-hand man? Kells will have my balls if I fuck this up. I turn from my ruminations back to the mess in front of me, and my phone buzzes. Fuck, can I not get ten minutes to myself? It's a text from Jordan, and a smile crosses my lips. My baby sister hangs the moon. Instead of texting back, I press the button to videochat.

"Bubba!" Her smile is huge on the screen.

"What do you want, Sunflower?"

She puts her hand to her chest as if she's offended. "What do you mean? I can't just text my big brother to make sure he's still alive when he's forgotten about me?"

I laugh at her dramatics and the lie. "I just talked to you two days ago, Jordan. You know some of us have to work for a living."

"Yep, me, and yet, I still find time to text you."

"Ha! How is the boutique?"

"Boring as hell!" she exclaims, exasperation in her voice. "Anyway, when are you coming home?"

I sigh, the need to stay and finish this work and help in the barn weighs on me. I get ready to tell her I won't be able to make it when I see the trembling pout in her lip. Dammit, I can't handle her tears.

"You're not coming? Not for either holiday?"

Tears well in her eyes, and I'm done. "No, I'm coming. I'll be home the day after Christmas. I have to cover some shifts in the barn. I need to come home anyway to get Taylor's friend who's coming to work with us."

"Oh yeah, that's right. Joanna's cool. She's around your age and owns a hardware store. She's pretty bad ass. Taylor works for her when she's not at the bed and breakfast. At least that's what she says. I think she's at the hardware store so much because she's fucking Joanna's dad."

I spit out the swallow of coffee I'd just poured in my mouth. "She what?"

"You didn't know?" she says, laughing at my sputtering, as

some of the hot liquid trickles down my throat and into my airway. "Yeah, he's a total hottie. Overprotective and maybe a little jealous, but absolutely fuckable." I choke on my own spit at the audacity of her this morning. "The twins take after him with the hotness."

Twins" is the first word I manage to say, though it's meant to be a question. "Jordan, behave yourself. What would mom say if she heard you talk that way."

"Don't act like you don't hear and say worse. And, yes, twins."

"I am a 34-year-old man, not my baby sister. Jesus Christ!"

"See!"

"Calling on the Lord is not the same thing."

Once she explains that Joanna is a twin and that Taylor is happier than she's been in years, I once again promise to be home in a couple days and get off the phone. That girl is going to be the death of me. I file away the need to talk to Taylor about her relationship choices and cringe at the thought of Jordan finally finding someone. She will likely give me a heart attack in that process. Either that, or I'll be in jail.

4

TOO LATE FOR THAT

*J*unior

Thankfully, the last two days on the farm are quiet, and I'm able to head to my parents' house as planned. Jordan texts four more times to make sure I'm still coming home, and my mom has called twice. I guess I created that monster with all the other family events and holidays I've missed during the active circuits. They just don't seem to understand my position and the fact I can't just take a vacation. I have a great team, but I'm the one responsible. I'm the one everyone looks for when something goes wrong, and something always goes wrong.

I had the presence of mind to send everyone's gifts early, which was a blessing in hindsight because I would not have had time to go shopping. Not only would I have not heard the end of it from Jordan, but dad would have pulled me to the side to verify the ranch wasn't running me into the ground. I can hear him now, *Son, you know that job will replace you tomorrow, but we can't.* I chuckle to myself. Mom and Jordan are the ones who insist on calling me damn near daily, but my pops is the worrier. I'm surprised he still has any hair between me and Jordan.

The six-hour drive flies by. It's unseasonably warm, and

though there's snow at the higher mountain altitudes, the roads are surprisingly clear for December in the foothills. I throw up a prayer of thanks because I don't have time to get stuck on this side of the mountains. I need to pick up Joanna and get back before next week. Rather than head directly for the house, I take the country road into Colliers Town as I pass through Cole County. Though I've never been to this town before, we've been part of the Eastern Rodeo Circuit since I joined the ranch as a hand nearly fifteen years ago. Cole County is where the Championship Run is held every year.

Taylor wasn't exaggerating when she said this town is still small. There's nothing more than a two-lane road in and out of the center of town. The downtown area looks like most old coal-mining towns with rows of store fronts and the occasional gas station. This one boasts two different brands and a few restaurants. I find JD Hardware easily enough and park in a spot out front. The storefront is clean and clear, and from what I can see through the window, it's well-stocked and neat. Maybe Taylor wasn't exaggerating about Joanna's organization and drive either. I sure hope not.

I grab my hat off the seat beside me and slide my coat on before stepping outside the truck. Though it's warmer than expected, it's still cold after having spent five hours in the heated cab. The last thing I need is to get sick. I realize I'm stalling when I stand outside the door rubbing my hands down my jacket. No sooner do I step inside after the door chimes than I'm attacked by an elf who barely comes to my chest.

"Reggie!"

Thankfully, I'm able to hold myself upright as both a cringe and a laugh overtake me, coming out as a snort. I wrap my arms around Taylor, pulling her head into my chest as tightly as I can until her arms are flailing. A cough comes from behind the counter, and I look up to see an older man staring daggers at me. He's shorter than I am, but he's burly as hell, like a damn wrangler.

That must be Joanna's father, the one Taylor's supposedly involved with. I loosen my grip a bit to let her breath, and she smacks at my chest.

"You still hit like a gnat," I say.

"I got your gnat," she retorts, and I barely twist my junk out of the way before her knee lands on my thigh.

"How in the hell do you manage to get them little legs up that high, T?"

She turns toward the counter and smiles at the man. "Oh, you know, lots of stretching," she says with a wink I barely catch before she looks back at me fully.

I roll my eyes. "You and Jordan are going to be the death of me."

"You'd miss us too much to die," she says, and takes my hand, pulling me toward the counter and the back of the store.

"Reggie, this is Garrett Daniels, my..." She pauses, looking up at him with a smile, "my boyfriend."

The adoration on her face is matched in the way he looks at her, like she is the sun. For the first time since Jordan told me Taylor was fucking some old dude, the rope around my chest at the idea of having to kill him for taking advantage of her releases. These two are in love like my parents are in love. Holy shit! My face beams with happiness for her, and I reach out a hand toward him.

"Call me Junior. T refuses to let me grow up, even though I'm damn near a decade older than her."

Garrett looks at my hand and then back at my face, trying to read me. He must see something that meets his approval because he finally takes my hand in his, giving it a strong pump. The squeeze shows a bit of his strength, but it isn't a power play, just a nod of authority. *Okay, old man. I see you.*

"I was worried when Jordan told me my adopted little sister had found herself a man. I thought I'd have to come around and defend her honor or some shit, but you're obviously doing something right to put that look on her face."

He raises a brow, and Taylor laughs. "A whole lot of something," she says.

"I don't need the gory details," I respond with a chuckle.

"Nice to meet you," Garrett finally says. He has a bit of a drawl that he doesn't try to hide, and I appreciate it. The man seems to be genuine enough.

"Are you on your way home?" Taylor asks, drawing my attention back to her.

"Yeah. I thought I'd come by and meet your friend Joanna before it's time for us to head back to the ranch."

I see Garrett's face draw up in a grimace. His body stiffens, and he turns away, walking through the door behind him. What is that about? I silently ask Taylor with a tilt of my head in the direction of his retreating back. She shakes her head sadly.

"Let me guess, he's..."

I don't get a chance to finish my statement when the door chimes that someone has come in behind me. I turn to see a tall brunette with curves for days standing just inside the door. She has strong shoulders, a long neck, and is wearing jeans that fit so perfectly, it's like they're painted on. I try not to stare, but my brain is going 'please turn around' on repeat. She also takes me in from head to toe. Her nose wrinkles in the most adorable way when she gets up to my face and hat. Maybe she's never seen a Black cowboy before. There are probably lots of people that have never been seen in this small town. I hold her gaze wishing I could read her thoughts and wondering how I can get her name without Taylor cock blocking.

"Just in time, Joanna. This is Regg...Junior Thompson," Taylor says.

My heart drops to my stomach, and my eyes go wide. This is Joanna? From the look on her face, she's equally as surprised as I am.

*J*oanna

You have got to be kidding me. The hottest man to have ever walked into my hardware store, standing there like a tall drink of water, is Taylor's friend? The one who offered me the opportunity of a lifetime? Fuck my life. I gather my wits about me at the same moment he reaches out a hand, a beautiful smile spreading across his face. Butterflies flutter in my stomach, and it's all I can do to swallow them down.

"Nice to meet you," I say, gripping his hand.

His grip is firm, and his hand is warm. I have to look up at him, which is surprising, as I'm usually one of the tallest people in the room around here, except, of course, for my pa and brother. I rarely wear heels because of it, even when I've gone out. Now, I'm wondering if they'd bring me eye level with him. I should not be so aware of this man if I'm going to work for him.

"The pleasure's all mine," he says with a drawl that makes me need to change my panties.

Shit, why didn't Taylor warn me he'd be coming today. Hell, why didn't she warn me I'd want to ride him more than any of the horses. *Damn. Shit. Get your head together, Joanna.* It's so hard to refocus when he hasn't released my hand. Thankfully, Taylor pulls us both back into the conversation.

"So what brought you here to Colliers Town again?" she asked, and I let go of his hand. My head tilts in curiosity of his answer.

He blinks down at me a few times before turning his attention back to her. "I didn't just want to show up out of nowhere..." *Too late for that, buddy*, I think to myself. "when it's time to head back to the ranch. I thought to introduce myself is all," he finishes, clearing his throat.

"That's very considerate of you," I say. A completely

unnecessary, but considerate gesture I doubt he's done with any of the other hands he's hired. "Do you normally roll out the welcome mat personally like this?" He laughs low in his throat, and those damn flutters are back.

"No. I always come home for the holidays, at least one of them. Since I was passing through, I thought I'd stop and check on Taylor and ask if you needed a ride to the ranch since we'll be heading in the same direction next week."

His eyes are intense, like he's waiting for a response to the unanswered question, and I swallow hard. Catching a ride would let me leave Pa the Mustang, so he wouldn't always need a ride from Jake. But catching a ride would mean six hours or so next to this man. I turn my attention to Taylor. "Where's my pa?"

She gives me a sad smile and cocks her head toward the stockroom door. Had he been out here and met my new boss. Was he uncomfortable meeting Taylor's friend? Something has to be wrong for him to have left Taylor alone out here with a man, especially a stranger.

"It's alright, Joanna. You don't have to decide today. Let me give you my number, and you can text me on New Year's Eve with your answer. I'll be leaving at sunrise on the first."

"Thank you," I say, my eyes still looking back at the storeroom.

"Go talk to him," Taylor says, and I take off in the direction of my office. Well, the office that's mine for the next four or so days.

I get to the door and pause. Turning back toward Taylor and Junior, I say, "I appreciate the offer, and I'll let you know later this evening or tomorrow. It might not seem like it in my surprised state, but I'm excited about the opportunity." I don't let him respond before I push through the door. I need to check on Pa and make sure he's alright.

5

IT'S NOT LIKE THAT

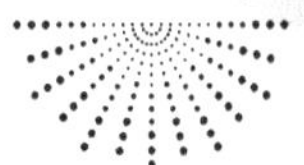

*J*unior

Five days off with my family is both exhilarating and exhausting. It is not, however, a vacation. Every morning, mom insists we all have breakfast together. Since Pops has to work every day between Christmas and New Year's Eve, that means we have to all be up and at the table by 6:30am. I might as well be back on the ranch. Like right now, she's downstairs banging around pots and pans. I'd be just as glad for a bowl of cereal around 9:30, but she's probably making pancakes and home fries. The likelihood of me still fitting into my Wranglers when I head back is slim.

"Get up, Bubba," Jordan's voice penetrates as she runs past my door.

Jordan has her own apartment, but she's opted to stay at home this week because I'm here. It's cute but annoying. By the end of day three, I'm wishing she had a boyfriend, so she'd have someone else for entertainment. Still, one more night before I grab Joanna Daniels and head back to the ranch, back to my normal level of exhaustion.

My mind turns to our new horsewoman, as it has every

morning since I met her. I don't know what I was expecting, but she wasn't it. Now, I'm about to spend six hours in the truck with her trying to keep things professional when what I really want is to invite her to my place for a bronc ride. Shit, these are going to be a long four months.

"Reggie, get down here for breakfast."

I drop both hands onto the bed in frustration. I'm not even hungry from how much she fed me yesterday. The crew will be laughing their asses off when I can't button my jeans tomorrow. I get up and slide on a pair of sweats I only wear to lounge around the house. That is exactly how I plan to pass the day. A little football, a nap here and there, and the ball drop at midnight. Then it'll be time to head back to the ranch.

"I was about to send your father up to check on you," my mom says when I hit the wooden floor at the bottom of the stairs. I walk into the kitchen and kiss her on the cheek.

"It's my last day off for a while, so I was..."

"Being lazy," my father adds in from his place at the head of the table. There's a smirk on his face.

"Not lazy, Pops. Strategically active. My brain was working while my body rested."

"And what were you thinking about up there?" Jordan asks, her voice far too cheerful for an early Thursday morning.

"All the things I left undone a week ago and everything new that's likely piled up. Also, everything I need to have in place for Joanna to settle in."

"Who's Joanna?" Mom's voice has a hint of interest in it.

Before I can answer, Jordan pipes in, and I close my eyes to keep from rolling them at her. "Joanna is Taylor's friend and boss who's moving to the ranch with Junior."

Mom's eyes widen, and my dad lets his paper droop a bit, so he can look over it at me. I shake my head and narrow my eyes at Jordan. As much as I love her, there are moments when she reminds me why people say that little sisters are a real pain in the ass.

"It's not like that. Taylor knew we had an opening for a hand to travel the circuit with us because of big mouth here. I offered to try her friend on for four-months. She's coming back with me tomorrow."

"Try her on?" Mom's eyes narrow, and I take a deep breath.

"Momma, it's not like that. She's never worked at a ranch or as part of a rodeo team. It might not be a good fit for her, so we worked out a temporary contract that could be extended."

A vision of her curves and strong grip flashes through my mind, and I immediately hope she'll decide to stay. I quickly take a sip of water to cool the rogue thoughts. Why the hell did I wear these sweats again?

"That reminds me that I need to run to Colliers Town today to go by her store and ask if she's going to ride in my truck or follow me tomorrow morning." I turn to Jordan. "Do you want to ride with me?"

Maybe if I take my sister, my parents will stop looking at me like I'm hiding a potential wife. They've been on me for years now, mom especially, to settle down. I'm perfectly happy with my bachelor life. I'm busy. I travel a lot. And I don't just want to marry a pretty face without substance or an interest in the same things I love. They want me to come home, and I'm not doing that, married or not.

"We can take a ride," Jordan says, a glint in her eye, "but you won't get your answer at the store." I tilt my head in question, and she laughs. "The store is closed today."

"Doesn't matter anyway," my father adds in, and I turn toward him dumbfounded by his statement.

"What does that even mean?" I ask, my voice rising slightly in confusion.

"We're going to Taylor's house tonight to bring in the new year," Jordan says matter-of-factly.

"What the hell does that have to do with anything?" I sit up straight in my chair, ready to rage at these vague and off-topic comments.

"Language," my father admonishes.

"Reggie," my mother, "the mediator", says quietly, "it means that you'll likely see this woman at Taylor's tonight if they are as close as you say."

I slouch back in my seat as my mind pieces together what they've been saying without actually saying anything. Taylor's having a New Year's Eve party. Joanna is Taylor's friend and boss. Taylor is dating Joanna's father, so, of course, Joanna will be there. My family is going.

"Wait, when was someone going to tell me we weren't just hanging out here for the new year?"

"We just did," Pops and Jordan say at the same time. They bust out laughing, and mom hides her laugh with her napkin. I close my eyes and stifle a groan.

6

YOU CAN DO HARD THINGS

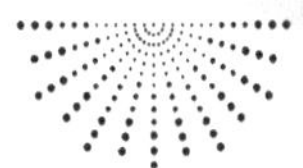

oanna Taylor has music playing at full volume as she putters around the house, dusting and rearranging. You'd think she'd never entertained before, though she's always worked in hospitality. Maybe there's something different about doing it as part of your job and actually having people in your home. I smile. She's made this town, and now this house, her home, and I couldn't be happier. I'd always stuck around because I was worried that no one would be here to take care of Pa, and now that excuse is gone. Taylor is everything he needs. A tear rolls down my cheek at the bittersweet thought that he doesn't need me anymore.

I look at the large suitcase and duffel bag on my bed. When I'd first told Taylor about my dream to join some kind of traveling circuit, so I'd not be stuck in one place again, it had been like opening the floodgates. I'd held back my own needs and desires for so long that I couldn't completely put them back in their locked trunk. Depression was settling in like it had never done before, so when Taylor told me to call Junior Thompson about a job, I jumped on it. Now, I can't stop staring at those empty bags. We'll

33

be leaving for the ranch in less than twenty-four hours, and I can't bring myself to fill them.

A soft knock breaks through my thoughts, and then Pa's voice penetrates the wood. "You alright in there, JoJo?"

I open the door and smile up at the man who's been both my hero and my heartbreak. His smile slips when he looks over my shoulder and sees the bags on the bed. I can't quite read the expression that's equal parts uncertainty, worry, sadness, and pride. It's a jumbled mess rolling across his face like a shiver. I look back in the same direction of his gaze and shrug.

"I've been staring at them for hours," I say quietly. "You're welcome to join me."

I step back and gesture for him to come inside, the music in the background a contradiction to the emotions swirling around the room. He takes a tentative step forward and then another until he can sit on the bed next to the duffel. He picks it up and runs his hand along the name stamped onto the thick hem—Daniels. I smile at the smirk that plays on his lips.

"Does Jacob know you're absconding with his duffel?"

"Nope." I raise my brow in a challenge, silently asking if he's going to give me away.

"I doubt he's going anywhere any time soon. He won't miss it, and maybe it'll help you not miss him," he muses, reading my thoughts without me having to say them.

"I don't know if I can do this, Pa." Emotion chokes my words off. "I need this. Lord knows I need to do this, but I can't seem to even bring myself to open the closet, let alone put anything in those bags."

"Baby girl, there is nothing you can't do. Everything you've done in your entire adult life has been hard."

I shake my head. I've taken the easy road with every decision. I did exactly what everyone expected of me.

"Don't shake your head at me, JoJo. You had the dream of leaving, but you stayed because it was expected of you. That was hard. Your husband was killed, and even though you were then free to move on, you stayed and played the grieving widow for years, ignoring your own thirst for life because that's what the town expected. When your ma passed..." His voice cracks, and I nearly break down in sobs. "When your ma passed, you took on the job of caring for me and Jacob, especially me. Putting all your wants and needs on the back burner is a hard decision."

I start shaking my head again. Leaving is so much harder. Can't he see that?

"I'm not saying the act of leaving everything you've ever known isn't hard. I'm sure it is, but you've already proven you can do hard things. You can do this, and you will do this. Now, open that closet door and start pulling out the things you need and want to take with you because if you don't, I'm sending Taylor in to do it for you."

"How dare you, old man? You'd threaten your own daughter with your mother-hen girlfriend."

"If that's what it takes." He winks, and his smile is contagious, even though his eyes still have a hint of sadness.

"Thanks, Pa."

He stands up and wraps his arms around me. I didn't know how much I needed this hug until the tension and fear releases bit by bit the longer he holds me. His acceptance of my dream and pride at my choice are enough to push me forward, but his hug seals the deal. It will be extremely hard to go months without a hug from this man, from anyone, but I will make it through because he believes in me.

7

YOU MUST BE FANCY

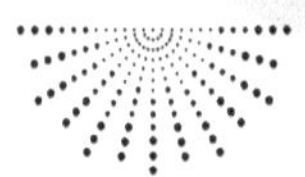

*J*oanna

We might as well have been having a Christmas party from the way Taylor had things laid out. There were cookies, teacakes, all kinds of finger foods, and holiday music blasting. She'd refused to take down any of the decorations, and the tree still lit the entire living space. I'd be lying if I said the entire scene didn't make me happy. Much like the impact Morgan's return had on our family, Taylor has brought this house back to life in a way I hadn't thought possible.

"What're you smiling at, JD?" Taylor asks, carrying another tray of food into the room and setting it on the table she'd expanded to its full ten-foot length.

I school my face into a stoic expression and look around before letting my eyes land back on her. "I was just thinking how this feels very Groundhog's Day." The questioning look she gives me nearly makes me lose my hold on the laughter. "You know, we're reliving Christmas around here." I widen my hands and twirl around, gesturing at the house. She rolls her eyes and then giggles.

"I don't want anyone sad about you and Reggie leaving tomorrow."

"Reggie?"

The look she gives me says I should know who that is, but before either of us can say anything more, the doorbell rings. I look back at her sheepish smile and narrow my eyes. Who else is coming that needs to ring the doorbell? Definitely not Jacob and Morgan. Taylor shrugs and goes to open the door at the same time Pa comes from the kitchen with a beer in hand.

Jordan steps through the door, passing by Taylor to give my pa a hug. He's laughing before she even makes contact. Where Taylor is sunshine, Jordan is energy personified. I've never not seen her in a flurry of some sort, like a constantly swirling storm that you just want to get caught up in. Behind her are an older couple, maybe a little older than Pa, who are definitely Jordan's parents. He's a little taller than Jordan but shorter than his wife. Jordan seems to have split the difference between them in all ways. She has her mother's beautiful cheekbones, smile, and warm mahogany eyes. Her complexion is on the darker side, even darker than Junior, whose entrance has caught my breath.

He has on dark-wash jeans that fit perfectly, a purple, button-down shirt with the sleeves rolled up to below his elbows, and a black Stetson. *Shit.* How am I supposed to work for this man when I can't stop staring at him? I don't look away quickly enough, and his eyes catch mine. Heat fills my cheeks before I realize he looks as uneasy as I am. What the hell does he have to be worried about?

"Let me introduce you to everyone here," Taylor says, breaking our focus. "You guys already know Jordan, and this is her family."

She starts to point out each person when my brother bursts through the door, two bottles of whiskey in his hands and Morgan at his back. He makes a beeline directly for me. "Here, sis, this one's for you!" After handing me the bottle, he finds Pa and gives him the other. "And this one's for you, old man. You're both gonna need it."

"Where's yours?" Pa asks in his deep tenor.

Morgan pulls a half-empty third bottle from the crossbody she's wearing. "He got the party started early, taking shots every time he thought about tomorrow morning."

A hush falls over the house as family and friends decipher the implications of her words. Morgan is the first to recover, and in true sorceress fashion, she brightens the mood.

"The house looks great, Taylor, and it smells divine in here." Turning toward the others, she extends her hand. "I'm Morgan, Taylor's boss and Joanna's best friend. The disruptive one over there is Jacob, Joanna's twin brother."

Taylor follows her lead and completes the introductions. Though they both smile warmly and hug me in lieu of a handshake, I get the feeling that Junior and Jordan's parents are scrutinizing me. Could they read my attraction to their son? Was I that obvious and out of line? I wish I could read their minds.

"It's very nice to meet you," I say in greeting before disappearing into the kitchen to catch my breath. This day has already been filled with far too many emotions, and I wasn't prepared for Junior and his entire family to show up here tonight. I certainly don't want to break down in tears in front of him before we even make it to the ranch. He might just change his mind.

"You aren't by any chance willing to share a shot or two from that bottle, are you?" A deep voice asks from the kitchen doorway.

I shrug and pull a couple glasses down from the cabinet. After pouring us both a healthy portion, I clink my glass to his. "Cheers to a new year and new beginnings," I say.

"To taking chances and seeing where the new year brings us," he responds. We both take a large swallow from our respective glasses before he gives me a salute and heads back out into the living room. I finish my drink and quickly pour myself another before I'm able to show my face again.

Liquid courage is a powerful thing. It helps me join the party when I'd rather hide in my room, and I'm able to enjoy the evening without breaking down in tears. We eat, drink, chat, and play games. Junior's family is really nice, and it's obvious they love Taylor as if she were a Thompson. As the midnight hour approaches, and reality begins to crash back in, I step out onto the porch to get some air.

At this time of night, the farm is dark, except for the light coming from the house and the stars in the sky. There are no close neighbors, so the night is quiet. I sit on the top step, looking out toward the dark barn. I miss the days when we boarded horses, when the farm was alive with animals, and the silence wasn't so oppressive. Pa says he wants to start bringing in boarders again, and I hope he follows through.

I don't bother to look up when the front door opens and the screen door closes. It's probably just Taylor or Jacob checking on me. My heart races when Junior's voice pierces the silence.

"Is this seat taken?" I shake my head, and he settles down next to me. "I thought you could use a refill." He holds a glass out in my direction. I take it with a nod of thanks and a small smile. "I imagine leaving your family and friends behind like this can't be easy, especially as close as y'all seem to be."

I give him a real smile then. "We are close, and no, it's not easy. It is what I need and want to do for me, but it's not easy. I hope knowing that doesn't make you want to change your mind about taking me on."

He shakes his head. "Not at all. I'd be more concerned if you told me everything I've seen tonight between you all was fake. I'd start questioning my own sanity. Well, maybe I sometimes question that anyway," he says with a wink that makes me laugh.

"Sanity is overrated," I say. He nods in silent agreement before commenting on how quiet the farm is. "I was out here keeping company with the stars before you joined me." He chuckles. "Yikes, that statement could probably have me committed, huh?" We both laugh aloud.

"I'll be right there by your side, I guess." He looks up toward the sky, and his gaze catches on something because he doesn't look back down. I follow his line of sight and land on the sprig of mistletoe hanging directly above our heads.

"Oh!" I exclaim, unsure what to say. I never noticed it up there before.

"I thought only fancy people hung mistletoe for Christmas. You must be fancy."

Heat rises up my neck, as I shake my head. "Not at all. I didn't even know that was there."

"Well, that makes two of us, so we have to follow tradition."

"Tradition?" I say, my voice cracking slightly. I don't know why I said it like a question. I know the fucking tradition of getting caught under the mistletoe.

He leans in closer to me, his nose nuzzling my cheek. Okay, maybe I'm just imagining the nuzzling because I can feel his breath on my face. I turn to face him fully, and before I can say anything, he presses his lips to mine. Both of our mouths remain closed, and the kiss lasts for maybe two seconds, but I know it's going to stay with me for far longer.

We pull apart right before the front door opens again, and Jordan calls us in to watch the ball drop. He stands and helps me to my feet. The night is nearly over, and the new year is already making promises it can't keep.

8

I'LL TRY HARDER

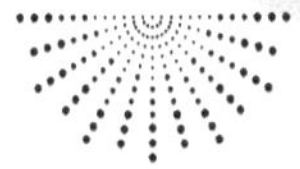

*J*unior

I wake with the feel of her lips still pressed to mine. There was nothing heated in that kiss, but it's clung to me. She was so guarded last night, and I don't know whether it was nerves because we're leaving today or that our family was there, but that one moment of quiet on the porch with her was perfect. She seemed to breathe a sigh of relief in the crisp air, and the smile on her face when I saw the mistletoe above our heads sealed the deal. I wouldn't have been a gentleman if I hadn't kissed her. When her eyes fluttered shut, there was nothing gentlemanly in my thoughts. Joanna Daniels is going to be a problem.

The smell of bacon and eggs hits me in the face as soon as I open my bedroom door. It's barely 6am on New Year's Day after we didn't get home until one, and, of course, mom is up cooking.

"Momma, you didn't have to make me breakfast this morning," I say, knowing she felt it necessary.

"Baby, you know I wasn't gonna let you go without taking something to eat."

I smile and drop my bag at the door before walking around the table to hug her. "I know, but I want to make sure you know I don't expect you to."

"And that's why I do it."

I smile and take a seat.

"We had a good time last night," she says after a few moments of silence while she carefully flips the eggs to a perfect over medium."

"We did," I agree.

"Taylor found herself a real nice family to join."

"Yes, she has. Jordan has been keeping me up on all the happenings with her every time she calls. I was a little uncertain about Garrett when she first told me their age difference, but when I saw them together, I could tell how much she means to him."

"You were ready to play big brother, huh?" she says with a chuckle.

"Whenever needed."

"You know, one day, Jordan's gonna find her match too."

I visibly shudder for her benefit because she expects it. "I know, and I will expect him to look at her like Garrett looks at Taylor, like Pops looks at you. Else, I'll put an end to it."

These conversations always start off the same. We talk about the girls, and she warms me up before turning the conversation to me and my lack of relationship. I play along every time, but I know it's coming. This time, though, she surprises me.

"Taylor really lucked out finding two women to work for who look out for each other."

"Jordan said they really have taken care of her and provided the support system she's needed."

"That girl needed strong and beautiful women in her life, so she could find her own strength and beauty. We sure tried to provide that for her every time she came around."

"Her life was rough," I say. Normally, I'm not one to gossip. I leave that to my mother and sister, but Taylor is like another daughter to Momma. "Did Jordan tell you that Garrett beat the shit out of Taylor's stepfather?"

"What? No, she didn't."

"Yeah. I mean, I wasn't sure it happened the way Jordan told it, but when I met Garrett and saw the way he looked at me for hugging her, I could see it. Definitely the protective type."

"I can see that," she says with her back to me as she puts bread in the toaster. "His son looks to be much the same way with how he looks at that Morgan.

I smile. "They're real nice people."

"And that Joanna," she says and then pauses.

I look up to see her turned around looking at me. "What?"

"She's pretty."

"She is," I agree because there's no point in lying. We all have eyes.

"She looked uncomfortable last night."

"Yeah, leaving is harder than she thought."

"Oh, I assumed she was excited to go."

"I think she is, and I also think she's a little worried about leaving her family and a little scared to leave home for the first time."

"For the first time?"

"Now momma, I don't know her life story like that, and we're not just gonna talk about her."

"I was just worried she was uncomfortable because we were there." The toast pops, and she turns back toward the counter to finish making breakfast.

"No ma'am. She relaxed out on the porch and told me she'd had a hard time packing her bags and getting ready to say goodbye. Maybe having her come right at the holidays wasn't a good idea. But from what I hear, she's got a lot of try in her. So long as she can withstand the pace of our work once we get on the circuit, she'll be fine. She won't have time to miss everyone."

"Oh, you mean like the weeks when you forget to call your

mother?" She holds the spatula out at me for emphasis. After a few seconds, she trades it out for a bag she sets in front of me.

I stand up to hug her again. "I'll try harder not to go that long," I whisper in her ear.

"There are sandwiches in there for you and Joanna," she says, and I smile against her shoulder. "Watch what you're doing." The shift in her tone is so unexpected, I pull back and look at her. "I saw the way you two watched each other last night. Just keep your wits about you."

A smirk forms on my lips. "I will," I say and give her one more hug before I head out the door. I had already said my goodbyes to Jordan and my pops before we went to bed earlier this morning.

Mom's not wrong about Joanna, but she's reading more into it than there is. Yes, she's beautiful, with curves to die for, or die in, but she's gonna be one of my employees. That means we gotta keep it professional. I just have to forget the feel of her lips on mine.

*J*oanna

I haul my bag out to the door only to find Taylor already in the kitchen with a coffee on the table for me and a Diet Coke in her hand. "You okay?" she asks in greeting.

"Good morning to you too." She purses her lips and raises a brow. "I'm good. It'll get easier once we're on the way." She smiles knowingly. She had more of a reason than I do to leave home, but the concern and fear at the process are similar, I imagine. "I feel silly, you know? Like I'm too old to be setting out and finding my way."

"You're never too old to find what makes you happy. Everyone deserves that."

She's right. I know she's right. I take a deep breath and then a sip of my coffee. "Pa still asleep?"

"Now you know better than that," she says. "He's outside in the barn. Whether he's trying to hide away or muster up the courage to say goodbye, I'm not sure."

Tears burn the backs of my eyes, but I take another sip of coffee and force them to stay in place. "Has he had his tea?"

"It's sitting right here waiting for you to take it to him."

I stand up and wrap my arms around her. "You have been a godsend to this family."

"Likewise, JD. Likewise." Her voice catches, so before we both end up blubbering messes, I grab the two mugs and head out to the barn.

"Hey, Pa, I brought you tea," I say on my way through the barn door. The last thing I want to do is spook him if he's as emotionally unbalanced as I am. I don't see him right away, so I call out again. "Where are you?" Nutmeg whinnies in her stable, and I head in that direction. "Where's he at, girl?" I ask the horse. She snorts out a puff of air and tilts her head to the side as if answering. I chuckle, rubbing her head softly before moving toward the last stable that used to serve as the boarding office.

Pa's leaning against his desk, staring at the photos and cards hung on the wall. So many of them are of Jacob and me with either Nutmeg or the different horses our family had boarded over the years. There are even a few of me with my old horse, Charity. The cards are from the various horse families, some of them thank-yous sent after they'd moved far enough away to have to board elsewhere, and others are old holiday greetings. I can't help but wonder if any cards came in after we closed the stable, and if so, what happened to them?

"It's not always easy coming out here," Pa says, startling me from my musings. "So many great memories captured in this space, and yet the fact that there's nothing left but memories hurts in ways I can't explain." I take a step forward, but he holds up a hand, halting my progress. "Just listen, okay?"

I nod before realizing that he won't see it facing away from me. "I brought you tea. You should probably take it before it gets cold. Then, I'll listen."

"Taylor sent you out here, didn't she?"

I snort out a breath, much like Nutmeg had earlier. "Not exactly, but she did have this cup ready when I walked into the kitchen."

"Of course, she did." He takes a sip of the tea and looks back at the pictures before addressing the elephant in the room. "Losing you is like losing your mother all over again." Before I can even respond, he turns his sorrowful eyes on me. "You can say whatever you like about how I'm not losing you, or how I have Taylor to take care of me, but neither of those facts takes the vise from around my lungs." With a weary sigh, he sits in the worn leather chair behind the desk. "I'm scared, JoJo. I don't want to go back to that dark place."

I hurry around the desk and wrap my arms around his neck from behind his chair like I used to do as a teenager. "How can I help, Pa?" I cringe at my pleading tone because I'm afraid he's going to ask me to stay. The last thing I want is that. I need to go, to find myself. Yet, if he says that the only way to keep him from another bout of depression is for me to change my mind, I know I'll be calling Junior Thompson with an apology.

His silence hangs in the air like a shroud that has me holding my breath. Several moments pass, though I swear it feels like an hour, before he grabs my hands and pulls me around to stand in front of him. "Look at me, JoJo," he demands when I keep my eyes averted from him, afraid he'll read my own fear in them. I swallow and finally meet his gaze. "It is not your responsibility to take care of me. It never has been. So, if you want to know how you can help..." I nod in the brief silence while he gathers his words. "Try harder to be happy."

My brows draw together. His words make little sense. Pa stands and turns me around to look at the wall he'd been staring it. I know every photo, ever award, yet I can't figure out the point he's trying to make until he raises his hand and points at the picture of me and Charity.

"That girl made decisions that made her happy in the moment. She was free and didn't give a damn about who didn't like it. That was the girl who made friends with Morgan when everyone else turned their noses up. That was the girl who told her parents she was going to marry her childhood sweetheart regardless of our feelings about it." He pauses again. "And that was the girl who disappeared soon after."

Tears leak from my eyes as I stare at sixteen-year-old me. I had been ready to take on the world back then, and I dared anyone to try and stop me. She got lost when I started worrying more about what everyone in town thought than what I wanted.

"Go find her, JoJo, and don't settle until you do."

9

I WILL BE

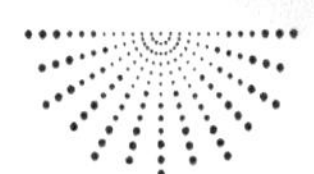

*J*oanna

Junior shows up at exactly 7:30am as promised. I had hoped he'd be late, so I could have a few minutes to brush away the sadness. I was also hoping that he wouldn't be a stickler for punctuality, as mornings have never been my favorite part of the day. I lost on both counts.

He's less put together this morning than he had been when he arrived for the party last night. He looks just as good, though, when he steps out of the truck to throw my bags in the back. Taylor and Pa step out onto the porch, and I lift my hand to wave. There's no need to bring on more tears by prolonging the goodbye. Junior walks up and shakes Pa's hand, and I watch the old man lean down to say something in his ear. I don't hear the words, but Junior's response creates a knot in my throat. "I will."

Once we're on the highway, Junior breaks the silence. "Are you alright?"

Do I tell him the truth? Say I don't know? I settle for the simple, "I will be."

We let the silence linger a little while longer before he speaks

51

again. "What can I tell you about the ranch that might make you feel less anxious?"

I snort out a little laugh. "I'm not nervous about the ranch," I say honestly. "Unless you all are some cannibals with demon horses I have to take care of, I'm not worried about the work."

"Then what is it? What is it that has you tied up tight as a baseball?"

"If you really wanna know, I'm worried about what I'm leaving behind and what I might come back to...if I come back."

"What made you decide to leave in the first place?"

"I've dreamt about leaving for years," I say quietly, my eyes trained on the road ahead of us. "Taylor helped me make the decision. She told me it was okay for me to think about myself for a while, that I deserved to find what would make me happy."

"That sounds like Taylor. She kind of did something similar herself not too long ago."

"How long have you been at the ranch?" I ask, trying to turn the attention from me.

"Honestly, my parents took me to the rodeo in Cole County when I was about ten years old. I fell in love with the horses and asked to go back every year, but they wouldn't take me. Their excuse was always that Jordan was too young." He shrugs. "I think they were afraid I might run into the corral and get trampled by one of the broncs, or maybe they were afraid that I would leave. Anyway, when I was sixteen, I got my first job and my car. I took myself back to the rodeo." I don't see his smile, but I can hear the change in his voice. "I started driving up to the ranch regularly without my parents knowing, and I got to find out about all the jobs available. I thought I'd be a rider, but I didn't want to give my mom a heart attack, so I got me a part-time job on the weekends working in the barn."

He turns to look at me quickly before putting his eyes back on the road, maybe to make sure I'm still awake and listening. He must've seen that my eyes were still open because he continues where he'd left off.

"When I turned eighteen and graduated from high school, I found out that one of the ranches in another county was hiring for a hand, and I took the job. I didn't travel the rodeo circuit with them, but I stayed there five years learning everything there was about taking care of the horses and managing the barn. They were happy to train me up, but they weren't willing to make me part of the team, so I came home for vacation during rodeo season and found another gig. The Doughertys hired me, and I've been with them ever since. It took another seven years with them before I became team manager, but I've loved every minute. Every season is just as exciting to me as the first. I think it's one of those things that if you love it, you love it, and you can never get enough."

At some point in his story, I had turned myself toward him to watch his profile. His voice is soft and compelling, drawing me in. I could've listened to him the whole ride, but he won't let me get away with that.

"Your turn," he says. "We have four more hours to kill. Either you talk, or I will turn on the radio and sing, and you don't want me to sing. I sound like a bull getting castrated by a wood chipper." I can't help but laugh at the description and almost want to dare him to do it. Hearing his story, however, pushes me to want to reciprocate.

"Taylor had been working for me for three months when she caught me in the middle of a meltdown in the storeroom." Though he's faced away from me, I can see his eyes widen and his head tilt. "Yeah. She had been yelling at herself about some thought going through her head, probably about my pa, and I told her I'd been asking myself something similar. Something along the lines of 'what the fuck am I doing with my life?'"

He gives me an encouraging smile, and I tell him about Jacob's broken heart and Pa's depression. I have no idea what it is about this guy that compels me to spill my life story, but I even briefly mention my marriage and the subsequent death of my husband. When he offers his condolences, I scoff.

"It wasn't a love match. I hate the fact he had to lose his life like that, but I was glad to be free of that expectation. I'd have never been able to go on this adventure," I say, gesturing toward the open highway before us, "if I were still married. Not to mention the fact, we'd have been miserable together. So, no condolences necessary."

He reaches over and covers my hand with his. "The wisdom of twenty years doesn't take away how hard that must've been in the moment." I look down at his hand, and he quickly pulls it away. My eyes snap to him, and he whispers an apology.

I smile reassuringly. "At any rate, once Morgan came back and then Pa returned to more of himself, I started thinking about my life and felt stuck. Taylor told me it was time to prioritize myself. So when she asked where I'd like to go if I left Cole County, I told her anywhere that would let me roam. With my fascination of traveling entertainment and experience with horses from our years boarding them at the farm, she suggested I talk with you."

"She called me and basically told me I'd be a dumbass if I didn't hire you on," he said with a shake of his head. "She can be a damn bulldozer sometimes."

I let out a full belly laugh. "Yes, she can." I sober after a few seconds. "I hope I don't disappoint you and let her down."

We both fall silent, the weight of our decisions heavy.

10

RUNNING TOWARD SOMETHING

unior

We both fall silent as the highway curves around the mountain. My favorite part of the drive back to the ranch has always been the moment Cole County disappears from my rearview. Though my family has always lived right across the county line, something about leaving it all behind makes me feel lighter. Today, though, things are different. Listening to Joanna's story, the little bit she shared with me anyway, has me realizing I've been blessed with a relatively easy life. Both my parents are still alive and healthy. Other than mom asking when I'm gonna get married and give her grandchildren, I've never been truly pressured to get married. Sure, I've had to work my ass off to get to the position I'm in now, but it's work I love, not obligation.

Joanna's face is turned toward the window like she's watching the world go by, and maybe she is. I use the opportunity to steal glances at her without her knowing. She's a beautiful woman. Long legs topped with thick thighs fill my seat, and let me not even think about the way her ass fills out those jeans she's wearing. The next glance has me wishing I'd have taken the opportunity to wrap my arms around her last night. Unlike most of the women I come into contact with, she's strong and yet soft in all the ways my body craves. Her eyes drift closed, and my eyes gravitate to her lips. I still feel... *Nope, stop that, Reg. She's your employee now. That kiss was nothing more than an alcohol-induced momentary lapse.*

"Shit," I say aloud when I realize I've drifted toward the shoulder thanks to the rumble strips shaking the whole truck.

"Wha...What happened?" Joanna asks, her voice shaky from being woken by my idiocy.

"Nothing, sorry. My mind wandered, and the wheels hit the rumbles."

"Do you need me to drive? I know we all went to bed late, but you had to have gotten less sleep than me with driving back and forth."

"Nah, I'm good. I was just thinking about what you'd said earlier about not wanting to disappoint anyone." I turn my face to look at her for a second before focusing back on the road. No need to have her questioning my driving abilities.

She turns her whole body to face me. "And why, pray tell, were you thinking about that?"

Though I'm not looking her way, I can feel the challenge in the question. The verbiage is something my mother would use if she were about to tell us how stupid our decisions were. *And what, pray tell were you thinking?* she'd ask, fully expecting neither Jordan nor me to have a good enough answer. Rather than try to make up something, I settle on the simple truth. "After listening to your story, I doubt you could disappoint anyone." The sound that leaves her throat is some form of a scoff combined with a sardonic laugh that might even accompany a sneer, but I'm afraid to look.

"If you had seen the devastation on my father's face when he found out I wanted to leave Cole County, you wouldn't think that. His disappointment was an anchor sitting on my sternum." She pauses for a moment, and I chance a glance from the corner of my eye to catch her staring past me at the passing landscape with a frown on her beautiful face. It's a solid moment before she speaks again. "I'm embarrassed to say that Taylor's fall, and the subsequent chaos of that day, were my only reprieve."

I reach out and place my hand on hers were it sits atop her knee. Her skin is warm, and I have to fight the urge to entwine my fingers with hers. I tell myself that she needs the comfort, but I know it's a lie. Something about her pulls me in, and the fact that she doesn't pull her hand away has me wondering if she doesn't feel the tug as well. Thankfully, she continues talking, which stops my thoughts from continuing to spiral in an inappropriate direction. I should not be feeling this way about someone who works for me, someone who might only be around a couple months.

"Though Taylor and Morgan have tried to tell me that I'm making the right decision for myself, I can't help but feel like I'm letting everyone down, like I'm somehow running away."

"It doesn't sound like you're running away at all. You waited until everyone important to you was taken care of before you left. The store is thriving and well-equipped to continue functioning in your absence. And you're following your dreams. None of that says running away to me. Instead, I think you're running toward future possibilities."

She places her other hand atop mine and squeezes before releasing my hand and turning forward again. "Is that how you felt when you left home for the first time?"

Ouch. Dismissed and asked to lay myself bare all in the same moment. Taking a deep breath, I give her the best answer I have. "I think it was a bit of both. I knew my parents were disappointed in my choice, but I also knew there was something more out there for me. My dreams weren't at home. They weren't going to be fulfilled through college or with a nine-to-five job." I pause, hoping she'll say something to keep me from spilling my embarrassing truth, but she doesn't. She sits there, silently facing forward and giving me space. "Sadly, I had to hurt them to make myself happy. I had to reject their dreams to find my own. Now," I say, my voice a little brighter, "they've gotten over it for the most part, except now my mother's fixated on other ways I've disappointed her."

Joanna's mouth drops open, but she doesn't say anything. I want to laugh at the response, but the fact she's surprised makes the situation that much more frustrating. I shouldn't be worried about disappointing my mother at thirty-six years old any more than Joanna should worry about disappointing her family. We're both grown and should be able to live our lives how we want, whatever that looks like.

We drive for another 30 minutes or so when her stomach growling breaks the silence. She slaps a hand over the offending body part, and I can't hold in my laughter. "I guess that's my cue to find somewhere to stop, huh?"

"Sounds like it. Taylor made us sandwiches, so a rest area works," she offers, and I'm grateful she thought ahead. I need to get out of this truck for a little while, even in the cool, mountain air. A little distance will do wonders.

*J*oanna

We stop at a rest area around lunchtime and sit at a picnic table eating the sandwiches Taylor packed. I smile at the thought of how much she has mothered me over the past few months.

"This is really good," Junior says with a satisfied moan.

"Yeah, Taylor has learned a lot in the months she's been working with Morgan. Now, Morgan's food is to die for." He eyes me curiously. "Seriously! If you ask my brother and Pa, they would both kill for her lasagna."

He opens his eyes wide, and I laugh. I was only somewhat

kidding. When he settles back into eating his sandwich, I watch him. I'm captivated by the way his jaw works and the way he licks his lips clean of any crumbs that might have dropped. The movement makes me think of last night's kiss and how its innocence shook me. Sitting here, I wonder what it would feel like to have that tongue glide over my lips. I jump when he clears his throat, a smile playing at the corner of his mouth.

"Are you just gonna stare at me, or are you going to eat your own sandwich?"

"Was I staring?" His smile spreads knowingly, and I try to tamp down the flood of heat trickling up my neck. "You know, the only way to truly know if someone is staring at you is if you're staring back at them."

He smirks and lifts his sandwich up to me in salute before taking another bite. I smile and return to my own lunch. Within thirty minutes, we're back in the truck and on the road.

"You know," he says, "I'm awfully curious what you were thinking about when you were staring at me."

"Oh really?" I ask in response, not willing to give anything away.

"Yeah. I was wondering if we were going to talk about that kiss last night, Miss Fancy."

I had just taken a sip of water and nearly choke. My gasp causes the water to go down my windpipe, and I start coughing so hard I double over. Tears run down my cheeks by the time I finally get my breathing under control and stop coughing.

"This morning, you said you all weren't cannibals, but is your plan to kill me before I even get to the ranch?"

He turns to look at me while keeping one eye on the road. I try to hold my expression before I start laughing hysterically. My emotions are all over the place today. Sadness, confusion, nerves, and maybe a tiny bit of lust. I won't admit to that last part though. He chuckles along with me.

"Not at all. Killing you never even crossed my mind."

The way he says that last sentence sends heat to my core. He's obviously thought of other things to do to me. Not for the first time since we met, I wonder just how closely we'll be working together and what this attraction to each other might mean.

GETTING SETTLED

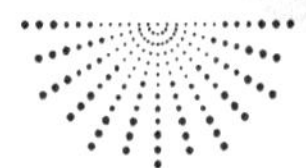

Joanna

Life on the ranch is nothing like life on the farm. I thought I knew what to expect because I'd spent so many years helping tend to the animals and working with the families whose horses we boarded. Our operation was nothing like this. There are more people working in the barn alone than have ever been on our farm at one time. The fact my eyes don't bug out of my head is a testament to the years of hiding my emotions. Also, thank goodness for Kelly Anderson, the barn manager, and Junior's right-hand woman.

With her help, I know the names of most of the hands and trainers who work in this barn. I also know all the Dougherty horses. I've not yet been trusted to help with others that are brought in for training from other places. There aren't many of those, though, so it hasn't been a big deal. Not having responsibility for more animals also leaves me some time to breathe, which is what I'm doing when Sterling Carrington approaches from the other barn.

I met Sterling during that first week when he was filling in for one of the hands in my barn who had gotten hurt somehow over the holidays. He seems like a nice enough guy and has taken it upon himself to show me around this part of the ranch during my lunch breaks. So, I'm not surprised to hear his drawl as I stand against the fence watching one of the trainers, Turner, I think it is, working one of the racing horses.

"Good to see I'm not the only one who likes to come out here and watch them move," he says, his deep gravel reaching across the open space.

I don't turn my head, simply respond with a "Nope, you're not alone there."

He sidles up and stands by my side, one booted foot up on the bottom rail of the fence and stays there for several minutes before speaking again. "Have you ever ridden?"

"A horse?" I screech, completely taken aback by the question. I'm literally here to work with the horses.

He turns to face me at my outburst, and the corner of his lips tilt downward when he takes in my expression. Then his ever-present smile returns, and he puts a hand on my shoulder. "No. I assume you've been on a horse before, else this is a strange job to have. No, I meant ridden as in raced?"

"Oh," I say, my voice and expression softening. "No, though I live in the same county as Boulder Ranch, which is the closest place to even see rodeo performances, we're still almost an hour away. Our farm just boarded horses, so I rode to exercise them, nothing more."

"No big dreams of being a rider then?"

"Nope," I say. I have no idea where he's trying to go with these repetitive questions, but I'd rather not waste my free time answering. When he doesn't turn away or look like he's about to leave me be, I turn the questions his way. "What about you? Big dreams of riding the circuit?"

"Nothing more than dreams. I took a pretty bad fall from a horse when I was a kid and have been afraid of heights ever since.

That fear doesn't work well atop a bucking animal that's leaping three feet further from the ground than I am tall."

"Yikes," I respond, holding back the very true follow up, *I wish I hadn't asked.*

"Don't look so crestfallen, Joanna. It wasn't really the fall that did me in. It was the pins in my lower back that kept me from riding for longer than I'd hoped. My seat has never been fluid enough again no matter how much I tried after I'd healed from the fall."

My mouth drops open further. Did he think that additional revelation was going to make me feel any better about opening up this can of worms? I start to say something, but his next words freeze the words in my throat.

"Seriously, no worries. You can make it better by joining me for dinner on Friday," he winks, and his wide smile does nothing to change my answer. "What do you say?"

I don't get a chance to respond when a voice comes from across the field. "Sterling. Don't you have work to do?" My eyes immediately snap to the origin of that voice like a bungee cord springing back into place. Junior stands outside the doors of the larger, practice barn, and damn does he look good. Sterling has also turned toward the barn, but my attention is locked on the man staring straight at me. When Sterling turns his head back in my direction, presumably to get my agreement for the date he'd asked for, Junior yells for him to get moving. "Charity's been waiting fifteen minutes for the horse she's supposed to be training, and you're costing us money," his voice booms.

Sterling takes in a deep breath and lets it out before walking off toward the front of the barn rather than where Junior is standing. It's probably a good choice because that man never takes his eyes off of me. We both stand there staring each other down like there's a tether holding us in place. Finally, the alarm I set to remind me of the end of lunch sounds in my pocket, breaking the spell. When I look down to pull the phone out to silence it, Junior disappears. *What in the world?*

Joanna

A few days pass, and I still can't get the intensity of Junior's stare out of my mind. He hasn't spoken to me since the day he dropped me off in the barn with Kelly nearly two weeks ago. In fact, she's the only person he'd introduced me to directly. It was like he was determined to get away from me. Truthfully, I've needed the space from him as well. Proximity to him makes me forget that he's my boss, and my mind replays that kiss on repeat. So, why would he stare at me like that when he can't be bothered to talk to me, to even check and see if I've settled in or not.

Admittedly, I've not given anyone much of a chance to catch me alone again since that day. The last thing I want is Sterling trying again to take me to dinner, and I sure don't need another staring contest with Junior. It's already hard enough when he penetrates my dreams. So, I've tried to keep my head low and my mind on the work. Most days, I do little more than muck stalls and brush down the horses after their practice. I stay with the group at dinner and immediately head to my room in the barracks when we're done for the day. Anything to keep my mind from wandering.

"Joanna!" Kelly's voice penetrates my wayward thoughts. "Where's your head at? You know that being around a horse's flank isn't a safe place to zone out."

She's right, dammit! I nod in acknowledgment, not having a better response. "Did you need something?" I ask. Kelly is a hard ass. I've watched her give a couple of the others a dressing down, and it's not pretty. For a woman who barely reaches five foot five, she's formidable, and I don't want on her bad side already. One of the things I've noticed, though, is that she appreciates others who are strong-willed and self-assured, so I keep my voice steady. She will not know I was daydreaming about our boss, or that I'm still feeling a little intimidated by the size of this operation and the sheer number of people here. I will do whatever is necessary to earn her respect. "I mean, do you need my help with something."

She stares at me for a long while as I finish brushing down Clementine before speaking again. "Yes, Junior asked to see you in his office. It's in the other barn at the far end." She must see my confused look and the way my eyes drift up to Clementine. "Finish with her first, and make sure her stall's clean, and she has fresh water. It won't kill him to wait." I fight to hold my mouth shut at her complete disregard of his position, but there's a glint of humor in her eyes. "Don't tell him I said that," she tells me. "Let me do it."

This time I do gape, but she just turns and walks in the opposite direction. Clementine's muzzle nudges my shoulder with impatience. "Ok, girl. I know you're tired of me holding you here," I say with a light pat to her side. She turns and tries to chew on my hair. "Stop that," I say playfully while pulling my ponytail out of her reach. "I am not a meal." When I'm all done with the beautiful creature and have her safely secured in her stall, I let out a long, fortifying sigh and head toward the other barn.

I CAN'T PRETEND

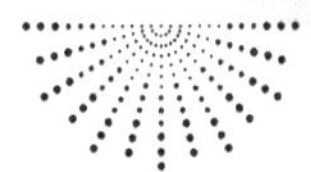

*J*unior
I spend the morning working on flyers for the exhibition ride we have planned for the end of next month. Every February, we try to put on a show for the locals who don't get to travel to the various rodeo locations. Maybe one day Dougherty Ranch will open up a showcase of our own, but that's not the direction the owners want to go right now, so we settle for a public practice run before going on the road.

I've already put advertisements in the local paper and will get these flyers posted around downtown this weekend. The first year of the show, we didn't do much advertising at all and had very few spectators. Most of them were family members of those who worked here on the ranch. Each year, though, it's grown, and we regularly have close to 150 people come.

A soft knock at the door pulls my attention from the flyers. I look up to see a beautiful face peeking around the door.

"Kelly said you wanted to see me."

"Come in, Joanna. I hope she didn't send you my way when you were in the middle of something."

"No, I just finished brushing down Clementine."

"Oh good. You don't look broken up, so she must be feeling better." Joanna's eyes widen a bit in surprised curiosity. "Kelly didn't tell you that she had a sore leg Christmas week and took one of our guys out of commission for a couple weeks?"

"My God, no!"

I smile sheepishly and gesture for her to take a seat across from my desk. I'm not quite sure what to say to her. I hate that I haven't check on her in nearly two weeks though it couldn't be helped. Something about her heats my blood, and after that six hour drive, I knew I would have to keep my distance. Still, I can't just pretend she's not here, especially since Jordan asks about her daily. Though it's probably because Taylor keeps asking her for updates, and I can't just keep saying she's settling in when I don't even know if she is or not.

"Did you need to talk to me about something?" She asks, pulling me from my thoughts.

"I just wanted to check in and make sure you're settling in alright."

"Everything's good. Everyone's been nice so far. It's a lot of work, but I don't mind the work. I hate the early mornings," she says with a shrug. "I won't lie about that."

I chuckle. I've always been a morning person myself, but I can understand the desire to spend a little more time in bed after a long day. "Have you gotten to know everybody?" As soon as I ask the question, I feel stupid. She literally just said that everyone has been nice. I stand up and walk over to the mini fridge against the wall.

"I think so, unless there are some people hiding in the woodwork or something. I mean, I think I've met everyone who works in the barn."

"Yeah, there are a lot more people on the ranch. I've been here all these years, and I still don't know everyone."

I turn around and find her watching me. "Are you staring again, Ms. Daniels?"

"No sir, just looking."

I turn back around really quick to hide the huge smile that breaks across my face. Kelly not only told me Joanna's proven herself a hard worker who loves the horses but that she also has a quick wit and a smart mouth. She doesn't let anyone talk down to her. The quick retort verified that observation and told me I wasn't the only one still feeling the attraction between us.

"Would you like a drink?"

"Are we allowed to drink during the workday, boss man?"

I choke on a laugh. "I wasn't talking about that kind of drink, but I'm sure I can find some of that too."

"Maybe later."

I swallow. "Maybe. For now, though, I got a couple different sodas and some water."

"Water's great," she says with a smile. It's subtle, yet it lights up her whole face.

I grab two bottles from the fridge and hold one out to her, letting my fingers linger when she grabs it from my hand.

"Do you have everything you need? I mean, have you really settled in?"

She thinks for a second. "I could probably use a couple things from the store, but I'm sure I can eventually catch a ride with someone."

A twinge of guilt settles in my stomach. I don't know what she might have needed, but in putting off talking to her, I kind of left her stuck.

"All you had to do was let me know, and I'd have taken you or gotten someone else to take you."

"You're busy. Everyone's busy. It's kind of the nature of the job, but I didn't think this far ahead when I decided not to bring my own vehicle. There's nothing I can't wait a little while longer to get anyway."

I'm undone by her patience and understanding. "How about this," I say, clearing my throat before I finish the offer. "I need to go into town to hang up some flyers for the exhibition we'll have at the end of next month. You can come with me, and we'll stop by the store."

"Sure. When?"

I had originally planned to get a couple of the hands to do the hanging this weekend because that's not something I wanted to do, but now that she's agreed to go with me, I don't want to wait for Saturday.

"How much more work do you have to do today?"

"Not much. I got a couple stalls to muck. The horses are being exercised right now, so I can get that done. Of course I'd like to shower before going into town," she says with a shrug.

"That's probably a good idea. I don't know if I'll want you in my truck if you don't."

"I'm sorry. Are you saying that you mind the smell of horses? Seems a little out of place for a man who's made a career of working with the animals."

I smile at her sarcasm, and with a smirk of my own, I respond. "I don't want a woman in my truck smelling like horses. I prefer she smells like a woman. Be ready to go at three o'clock."

I sit back at my desk, silently dismissing her. I need to get the flyers finished and printed, and I only have a couple hours to do so. As soon as she's out the door, and it clicks shut, I run my hand across my hard cock and will it to go down, so I can get to work.

13

CHOCOLATE, ICE CREAM AND TISSUES

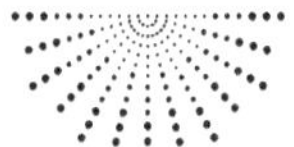

*J*oanna

Time seems to fly by before we're in Junior's truck heading into town. There is a stack of flyers on the seat between us like a wall. I pick one up and read the events listed. Roping, Rustling, Bucking, and Racing. I snort trying to hold back a laugh. Junior cuts his eyes in my direction, and I cover the huge smile on my face with my hand.

"Something funny?"

At first, I shake my head, but his look, combined with the headline, pushes me to laugh aloud. I point at the paper, and he looks down before turning his eyes back to me with a question knitted into his furrowed brow.

"That's seriously the title you're going with? No catchy name, or something with the word 'Showcase' or 'exhibition' in it?"

"People around here like to know what they're getting into it. They already know who we are, and we've done this for a few years now," he says with a shrug, but there's uncertainty in the gesture.

"Maybe so, but you could grab a few others passing through if you gave it a fun name and had food trucks or other fun stuff. Make it a real family event for the community. Of course, it's still just going to be Dougherty Ranch, but it might show how the ranch is growing and putting this little town on the map. Better than the three Rs and a B." I return his shrug.

He gives a small, noncommittal 'hmmm' before turning his focus completely back to the road. Of course, once I get a thought in my head, though, I cannot just let it go. "It could be a full day-on-the-ranch type of thing for families—some daytime events, maybe a petting zoo with the other animals, and a meet-and-greet with our performers, animals and humans." I'm working out logistics in my head as I watch his jaw tick. Does he hate my ideas or just the fact that I'm sticking my nose in where it wasn't invited? "No need to stew. You could just say no."

His head jerks around to me so quickly he pulls the wheel along with it and has to correct himself back on the road. "What? I'm not stewing. I'm thinking," he says emphatically, turning his eyes back to the road again.

"So, your jaw ticks like that when you're thinking? You looked pissed."

"When I'm concentrating, yes. My tongue works the inside of my cheek. Been like that since I was a kid."

Warmth spreads up my cheeks as I imagine the work of his tongue. That thought is definitely not kid-like. A smile once again spreads across my face as I try to hide my heated expression.

"What?"

"What do you mean, what?"

"What're you smiling about now?"

"Aren't you supposed to be watching the road and not me? You already just about ran us into a ditch."

"I am watching the road."

My brow lifts. "Then how'd you know I was smiling?" His lip quirks up, but he doesn't answer. I ignore his attempt to derail the conversation. "So, what were you thinking about before?"

He sits silently for a few moments as we enter the patch of civilization that seems to be surrounded by farmlands for as far as I can see. "Your ideas. We might do well to expand the event a little, really get the community behind Dougherty Ranch. Seems like I wasted my time on these flyers then."

"Not wasted, just a little teaser. We'll put these up strategically for the locals, and then you can make some others to put up in more public places coming in and out of town from both sides."

"We," he asks with a grin after pulling into a parking spot in front of the local library. Before I can respond, he tips his head toward the building. "Let's start here and then walk our way up one side of the street and down the other. You know how small towns are."

"I do, indeed. Now, what did you mean by we?"

"Oh, you can't just throw ideas like that out on the country-road drives and think you're not going to put in any of the work to make them happen? No ma'am."

I playfully slap my hand against his shoulder. "Don't ma'am me. We're near the same age." I climb out of the truck and walk around the front to meet him on the sidewalk.

"'Ma'am or Mistress,' take your pick, but I promise that 'Yes, Mistress,'" he drawls out slowly, "will get a lot more interesting looks from those around than 'Yes, ma'am.'"

If it were possible for a person to melt into a puddle of water like in *The Wizard of Oz*, I would be on the ground waiting for flying monkeys to splash all over me. Fuck, this man is dangerous. We've not even been in town five minutes, and I already need a change of panties. I clear my throat trying to buy time to develop a response. When nothing comes out of my half-open mouth, he chuckles and walks toward the front door.

Thirty minutes later, we've talked to some of the townsfolk, posted ten flyers on public-facing message boards, and asked some of the locals what they thought might improve the event. Many of them liked my idea of a meet-and-greet. Because it was mid-week, there weren't many younger families, or rather families with younger children to ask about the petting zoo, so we left that one alone.

At the market, we pick up the few items I need. Thankfully, his relationship with Jordan makes me buying feminine products a lot less awkward than it might have been otherwise. Our Ma did a great job of prepping Jacob to be a good partner in that arena, and it seems that Junior's parents were open with him as well. I nearly laugh aloud when he asks at normal volume whether I like to plug it or pad it. When an older woman smiles at the two of us, he wraps his arm around me and asks whether I want ice cream or chocolate. She passes by and taps his arm. As soon as he leans down, so he's at ear level, she whispers conspiratorially, "Get both and some Kleenex. The good kind with the lotion, so she doesn't chafe her pretty face."

"It is a pretty face, isn't it?" She nods, and with a wink, she leaves the aisle.

I hold my hands under my chin and mimic, dropping my voice slightly, "It is a pretty face, huh?"

"Yes..." he pauses for a second. "Yes, Mistress, it is."

The laughter that had bubbled up gets caught in my throat as heat creeps into my ears this time. He walks away chuckling. "Let me get us a buggy, since we now need chocolate, ice cream, and tissues."

14

STIFF JEANS AND WET PANTIES

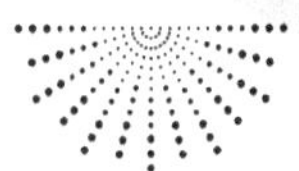

*J*unior

I have to walk away from her. I need to stay away from her. Yet she'd felt so good pulled against me with my arm around her shoulders that every fiber of my being wants her back there. The scent of her citrusy shampoo has taken root in my nostrils, and my lips twitch at the thought of running them along her jaw to her ear. She may have been the one to turn red, but I'm the one having to walk off this stiffness in my jeans.

Whatever is getting into me about her needs to work its way out. Not only should she be off limits, but even the encouragement of her ideas for expanding the exhibition is more than should be allowed. I need to run the idea past the owners. The more I think about it, though, the more I nix that thought. The Dougherty brothers aren't interested in expanding anything or changing anything. It had taken months for me to get them to agree to the first exhibition, and they've barely cracked a smile at the improvements we've made each year. They're very happy with the status quo. So long as the animals perform and are taken care of, they don't want any of the fanfare. Nope, I'll make the executive decision and pay the piper later.

83

By the time we get back to the truck, its dinner time, so we throw everything in the cab and walk over to the small diner that has the best burgers in town. She tells me about how Taylor came to work for her and the details surrounding her father's relationship with my adopted sister. For all her snark and dark past, that girl could worm her way into anyone's heart with her bright personality, and even brighter wardrobe. We both laugh at Joanna's description of Taylor's outfit that first day she'd entered Colliers Town.

"Those clunky shoes were my sister's doing. She'd bought them from that boutique she works at near the university. I think she gave them to Taylor for her birthday last year."

"Well, they made an impression, that's for sure. I have never in my life wanted to stand out that much. I lay back and watch from the wall, hoping I blend in. I've never wanted the spotlight."

I look at her dumbfounded. "Really?" She nods, quickly popping a fry into her mouth after dipping it in a mixture of mayo and ketchup. "Why, Miss Fancy, I'd have thought for sure that you dominated a room."

She stiffens for a second, enough time for her cheeks to turn pink, before she responds with, "Decimated is more like it. I've always been more like a bull in a tea shop, or however the saying goes. I never really learned the art of subtlety or southern nicety. Morgan's the hostess. I'm the muscle."

"What about your brother?" I ask, allowing her the moment of denial. She definitely garners all of my attention.

"Oh, Jacob's the peacemaker, except when it would come to someone fucking with me or Morgan. The only time he ever fought were some boys trying to bully her. It was a real surprise when he decided to join the military. He'd have hated combat." She falls silent for a few moments, like her mind has run away from her. "Anyway, that's why I was content running the hardware store and why I love working with the horses. Horses are easier than people."

I want to ask where she'd gone, but I laugh instead, a genuine chuckle at the veracity of her statement. "That's the God's honest truth right there. Speaking of horses, do you think Clementine's in good spirits enough for an exhibition?" She gives me a broad smile.

"She's the sweetest. If she was hurting a few weeks ago, I'd have never known it. Maybe Jerry just rubbed her the wrong way."

"No pun intended," I interject.

"Oh, all pun intended," she retorts with a bright laugh that makes my stomach clench.

"How'd that laugh alone not draw all eyes to you?" I say before my brain can stop me.

"I'm sorry."

"No, I'm sorry. That was…" I cough trying to come up with a way to finish this sentence with my ego intact. "unprofessional." I wrinkle my nose at how wholly ridiculous that statement sounds even to myself, and she tilts her head.

"Well, we've been talking about some pretty personal stuff all evening. I mean, you helped me pick out tampons."

Joanna

There's something about the hint of embarrassment that crawls up his cheeks, giving him a warm glow. Warmth crawls into my abdomen and takes wing at his words, so I have to break the spell. Let's be clear that he is weaving a spell over me, and that can't happen. I'm too damn old for fairytales. Besides, no one ever warned me that the handsome prince would be a cowboy in well-worn jeans.

He finally breaks the tension with a quiet chuckle and an even quieter 'touché' in his deep drawl. "Let's head back," he offers. I don't really want the evening to end, but I agree. At the end of the day, I still have a 5am wakeup call that does not care about my interest in spending time with this man. So, what makes me turn back toward him when he opens the truck door for me, I'll never know.

"By the way, cowboy, the pink that flooded your cheeks back there was cute."

He stands stock still barely blinking for a few moments before gathering his wits enough to retort, rather lamely, "I don't blush."

"Oh, but you do," I say, reaching up a hand to rub my thumb across the apple of his cheek. The change that comes over him this time is heated but not with embarrassment. His pupils dilate, only visible because of the well-lit parking lot, and his mouth opens slightly as he presses into my palm. Fuck, the way he's looking at me has my breath caught, the moment holding.

When he presses into me, bending my arm up between us, not letting me break our contact, I gasp. And when he snakes a hand around my waist, pulling me closer yet, I grasp his shirt like a lifeline. "What is this spell you're weaving, woman? This urge to know you, to touch you, to kiss you." With that last word, his head dips down, and our mouths meet, my neck craning to avoid the brim of his hat bludgeoning my forehead on instinct.

Unlike our chaste kiss under the mistletoe those weeks back, this kiss is liquid fire. Desire pours from his lips, and I melt into them. If my panties hadn't already been ruined before, they are destroyed now as my arousal takes over. I lift my hands up around his neck and pull the hat off his head, so I can get a better angle. I pull him in closer, dancing my tongue with his until his hands grab ahold of my ass and lift me off the ground. With a whimper, I wrap my legs around his hips.

The spell breaks when a car door slams. He looks into my eyes, and I watch the fog of lust clear before I unwrap my legs from him, and he releases me completely. Shit, was I really just humping this man, my boss, in the middle of the library parking lot? He takes his hat back from my hands and gestures for me to get in the truck.

"We really ought to get back."

Silence fills the truck on the ride back to the ranch. Silence and uncertainty. I spend most of the ride looking out the window or down at my hands to keep from staring at him. I refuse to regret what just happened. In fact, I try not to think about it at all. The only problem is the subtle reminders won't let me forget. His scent that still wraps around me. The strength of his hands that are gripping the steering wheel so tightly, I'm surprised he hasn't pulled it off already. And these fucking wet panties.

15

AN OPEN BOOK

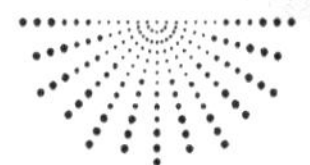

*J*unior

The weekend creeps closer, and I'm reminded at every turn that the exhibition date is quickly approaching. We still haven't created the advertisements or planned for the rest of the events. *We. Fuck me. There is no we.* There's the ranch, and there's the showcase. There's also the rodeo circuit. There are responsibilities to prepare for, but there is most definitely no we. I'm pulling my curls loose when a knock sounds on my office door. Plopping my Stetson back on my head, I invite whoever it is to enter. I sure could use the distraction.

"Got a minute, big man?"

I chuckle at nickname Kelly's chosen to call me and gesture for her to have a seat in one of the chairs across the desk. "You're not going to let that go, ever, are you?"

"Hell no! Play stupid games, win stupid prizes, and you earned that name."

"And the damn scar that came along with it. That wasn't enough of a trophy?"

"Nah, you can hide that one," she says with a smirk.

Kelly's one of the few people in the barn who's been here

almost as long as I have. The others from my early years have moved on to other ranches or left the scene altogether. I'm too damn stubborn to not see this thing out, to not see this ranch grow to the biggest name in the rodeo association. We have everything we need to stand out, except ambitious owners. They're happy with the mediocre bragging rights from our wins, but they can't see how much more we could do if we offered opportunities that would bring others to us.

"Earth to Junior. Thompson, Double D's got a problem."

"Huh, what problem? Is everything alright?"

She laughs aloud, and I realize that she meant I'm the damn problem. I scowl, and she laughs harder.

"Where the hell is your mind at today, Thompson?"

"Same place it always is. How to build this ranch into a showstopper."

"You've gotten us further than the Doughertys have ever been before. Celebrate that! Then, push a little more and a little further. You got my support and the support of at least half the barn. I bet if I asked, you'd have the support of the bulldoggers and wrestlers too. Just because the big house is content doesn't mean those of us doing the work aren't behind you."

"I just gotta figure out how to make them see the value in giving a little more effort, opening the door just a little bit more."

"You will. You told me that you had an idea to expand the showcase to bring in more people, maybe even some out-of-towners."

"Not me. Joanna. She had some ideas when we went into town the other day."

"And...have you got them in place? What do you need?"

I take my hat off and lay it on the desk before pulling at my coils again. I could stand a shape up, but I don't feel like driving into the city. I see Kelly's brow raise and realize I've been silent far too long.

"We haven't worked through the details yet."

"What in the hell're y'all waiting for? The day'll be here before you know it."

"Some of us work, you know? She's new, and you know you're hard on the newbies, and I'm well…" I trail off, unable to say the thoughts really flowing through my mind. The ones that say I'm trying really hard to keep her out of my head. I'm fighting the urge to bend her over a hay bale in the loft. The thoughts that keep me up at night fisting my cock. Instead, I finally finish with, "I've just been busy getting us ready for the circuit."

Kelly eyes me suspiciously but, thankfully, doesn't press the issue. "Well, this hard ass must've had a soft spot because Joanna finished up early today and took off for a ride up the Chickasaw Trail. I'm sure you could catch her to chat if you left now. It's not like you looked really productive when I came in here, and your hair could use a break."

I released the coil I had wrapped around my index finger with a sheepish grin and put my hat back on. "I guess I could use a break, huh?"

"Looks like it. Take Apple. He's not been worked today."

I stand, drop a couple waters in the saddle bag I keep on the stool behind my desk, and head for the door. "I hate that you can read me so well."

"Stop leaving your dog-eared pages open, and it might be a little harder."

I step over the threshold before turning back to my barn manager with a quizzical look. "Has Joanna had a tour of the grounds yet?"

"Nope, but she's a damn fine horsewoman. I wouldn't have let her go if I didn't think she could handle it. Still, it wouldn't hurt to have a guide if that storm on the horizon heads this way."

"Shit," I say aloud, already turning in the direction of Apple's stable. I don't bother asking which horse Joanna took. It doesn't matter. Apple knows this land like he'd been born on it, probably because we bought him as a foal. We've only recently had him gelded, and he's become one of the most popular horses for trail riding.

"C'mon, boy, let's go for a ride," I say to the beautiful mustang when he nickers as soon as I open the door to his stall. I take a moment to look around at the doors that are open and notice Clementine's stall is empty. "She couldn't have," I say aloud, and Apple snorts. "She wouldn't, right? Kelly wouldn't have let her... right?" Still, an urgency to find her fills me. Not only is Clementine one of our top performers, I'm still not convinced she isn't recovering from some kind of injury. There's just no other reason she would have kicked Jerry. Except Joanna's words penetrate my musings. *Maybe she just didn't like the way he touched her.*

Nope, not going to let my mind go there. Not going to think about how much Joanna seemed to like the way I touched her. No, absolutely not. Not going to think about how fucking much I liked the way she touched me. Those thick thighs strapped around my hips. No. I will not think about that or the weight of her perfectly plump ass in my hands. "Jesus," I breath out and rearrange myself before swinging onto Apple's back.

*J*unior

Twenty minutes on the trail, and I still haven't come across Joanna. *Where the fuck is she?* She doesn't seem like the adrenaline junky who'd veer off the trail for an adventure when she doesn't know the terrain, and Clementine knows this land almost as well as Apple. She'd steer her in the right direction. *I hope.*

Each new fork in the trail has me looking around, trying to identify anything that will show the direction she's taken. I have to trust that she's actually followed the trail, and maybe she's made her way faster than expected. Kelly did say Joanna was a fine horsewoman. Maybe she pushed Clementine harder than a novice would have…or than any of us who know her value would have. That thought gnaws at me for the next leg of the trail. What a reckless decision to bring our championship horse out here, especially with a storm coming.

Wait, does she realize there's a storm coming? Maybe that's why she's pushing so hard to finish the trail. I let out a shaky breath with that thought. It makes much more sense than to think she'd diverge from the trail and take off on her own. At the top of the trail, I turn to look toward the horizon, and fuck if the clouds aren't rolling in much faster than expected.

"Ok, boy, let's make our way back down. You know the way, and I want to get back before the brunt of the storm hits us. Either we'll catch up with them, or they'll be back in the dry barn before we even get there." Apple snorts, and I take that to mean he agrees, but he doesn't move when I pull him to the left toward the downward trail. "C'mon, boy. Let's go!" I pull the reins a little harder, but he doesn't budge. On the contrary, he nudges right. "No, we're not going to the cabin right now. That storm's rolling in, and we'll be stuck up here for hours if we don't get back down the trail now." I don't have time to sit here arguing with a fucking horse. Another glance toward the horizon has my heart pounding. The clouds are cresting the tree line, and they'll be over us in no time. Apple pulls to the right again, and grudgingly, I let him take the lead.

As we reach the tree line leading to the overlook, I notice some fresh tracks. Someone has been up here recently. That doesn't make any sense. No one comes up here but me. Apple whinnies, and I narrow my eyes. No sooner do we break through the trees than I spot them. Clementine is standing along the edge of the ridge that looks out on the ranch. On the other side of her stands Joanna. She's not yet noticed our approach, which means, she likely hasn't noticed the storm either.

16

DANGEROUS TERRITORY

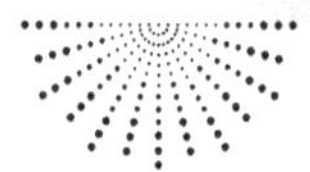

*J*oanna

God, I miss riding. It's been years now since I had access to horses that were still rideable. Jacob's old mare hasn't been able to carry anyone in years, long before we sold off the rest of the horses and closed the boarding stable. This level of freedom is exactly what I've needed.

It's not that I don't like it here on the ranch; I do. And it's not that I even feel out of place like I don't belong; I don't. It's just that I feel stuck. I guess in a way, I am because I left my car home. I can't just take a drive and get away. This, however. This trail. This horse. This moment has me feeling more like myself than I have all month. Well, except for those few hours the other evening.

No, I don't need to conjure Junior or relive that kiss. I don't need to remember it because it's never left me. I just need to keep riding until I forget. When the path seems to split at the foot of a huge oak, I nudge Clementine to the right, but she pulls left. "C'mon, girl, just a little extra trail. I'm not ready to head back yet." She shakes her head in chastisement. "Please," I say aloud, as if the whole idea of me begging a horse for permission to take a longer ride isn't ludicrous. I lead to the right again, and finally she relents with a sigh. *Judgmental ass horse*, I think to myself and laugh.

Twenty minutes later, we come to an open field that leads to a ravine overlooking the ranch. The land goes on for miles, and there are multiple barns out to the west away from where we care for the horses. Not wanting to be atop Clementine along the edge of the ravine in case something should frighten her, I drop down to the ground and look more closely at the landscape set out before me. It's stunning.

The sound of an approaching horse brings my attention back to the clearing. Any nervousness I might have felt dies when Clementine whinnies in greeting before the horse and rider even clear the trees. "I know what you mean," I say to her when my heart does its own little whinny at the sight of Junior atop the mustang. He was made for the saddle, his body loose, and his movements one with the horse as they both saunter our way. When he slides off the horse's back, I bite my bottom lip at how smooth his movements are and how the muscles of his chest and shoulder flex. Damn, he is sex on a stick.

"Joanna," he drawls at the same time his horse nickers in Clementine's direction. Junior looks back at the horse and shakes his head. "No balls, and you still can't behave yourself around her, can you?" I'm so taken aback by the statement that I can't keep from laughing uncomfortably. "What?" he says, addressing me. "We had to have this damn horse gelded because he kept trying to mount her. He damn near broke out of his stall three or four times while she was in training."

My laughter takes over until I'm bent over wheezing. "You're telling me that he acted just like a man, and you cut off his balls," I manage to wheeze out. "Sounds like we're handling things all wrong when it comes to humans."

"Well, it does sound like an apt punishment for a man who tries to take advantage of an unwilling woman," he says as he steps closer to me. "Clementine doesn't seem as unwilling as all that, but we couldn't let him ruin her career."

I tilt my head up to maintain eye contact. "Are we still talking about the horses?"

He nods down at me and mouths the word yes. The sight of his tongue peeking out between his teeth leaves me breathless. "We could talk about other punishments, though."

My brows furrow and I purse my lips. "Such as?"

"Such as the punishment for a woman who," he pauses and licks his lips, "makes her own path through unknown territory without any thought for her own safety or that of the prize horse she's riding."

I take a step back. "What do you mean? I followed the trail."

He shakes his head. "This isn't part of the trail, Fancy. You left that back yonder. This is private property."

"Isn't it all private property?" I ask in my snarkiest tone. "This whole damn ranch belongs to someone."

"Yes," he says, stepping back into my space and bringing my chin up with his index finger, "but this plot of land belongs to me. If you'd have gone a little further on the other side of that clearing, you'd find a small cabin. This is where I plan to build my house."

My jaw drops, and I try to form words. I knew he didn't stay where the rest of us did, but I didn't realize he had his own home here on the ranch, his own plot of land. Before I can say anything, though, a clap of thunder crashes, causing us and the horses to jump. I look around for the trail back to the barn. By the time I grab Clementine's reins and begin to walk in the direction I think we came from, rain droplets create dark circles on my shirt. It had been an unseasonably warm day, so I hadn't bothered with a jacket.

Before I walk ten feet, Junior's hand wraps around mine, and his arm rests on my shoulders, leading us in the opposite direction. "Where's your jacket?"

"I didn't bring one."

"No hat either?"

I shake my head, my hair already sticking together thanks to the increased rainfall. He shakes his head at me, disappointment dripping from his expression like the water now dripping from the rim of his Stetson. He pulls it off his head and drops it onto mine. The gesture sends a flurry of butterflies into my belly.

"We won't make it back to the barn before the storm pummels us, not as fast as the rain is picking up already." No sooner has he finished the sentence than lightning flashes across the quickly darkening sky, followed even more swiftly by a loud clap of thunder.

"We can't just hang out in the forest."

"There's a cabin, remember? And a lean-to that will protect the horses. If something happens to Clementine, Kelly will kill you, and she'll likely take me out as well just for spite."

We pick up the pace, and I let him take the lead when we get to a narrow trail between the trees. He wasn't lying that there's a cabin not fifty feet from the tree line. It isn't the tiny, one-room-schoolhouse looking edifice I was expecting out here on the edge of the ranch. Someone had clearly taken pride in building it and making sure it's comfortable. There's a fully fitted door, multiple windows along the front, and a generator sitting along the outside wall next to a woodpile.

"Go on inside," he yells over the next thunderclap. "I'll secure the horses."

"I can help."

"Go." He points in the direction of the front door and then turns to walk around toward the back of the cabin.

I want to stomp my feet in protest, but the rain is already soaking through my shirt, and I do not need to catch pneumonia from an ill-timed winter storm on what was a beautiful day. I sigh and make my way up onto the porch.

As soon as I open the door, I'm transported to another place. As rustic as the small house looks from the outside, it is just the opposite inside—modern and comfortable. He has a home office area set up along one wall near the kitchen, and it appears to be a fully rendered kitchen, complete with a fridge and tap. *Is there running water up here?* The furniture is made for comfort, like he wants this to be a space he comes to for relaxing, unlike the heavy mahogany that decorates his office in the barn.

A chill runs up my spine, and I make my way to the wood-burning stove that sits between the small dining table and the kitchen. Wood is already sitting in the small hearth, and matches are within easy reach, thank goodness. I get the fire going and turn around to let it warm my back before closing up the opening, letting the heat steep into the rest of the house.

The door slams open, and Junior stands on the threshold dripping from every inch. He is drenched, and when he wipes water from his eyes, guilt gnaws as I realize I'm still wearing his hat. I slowly reach up and take it off my head, holding it out to him like a peace offering. He takes his jacket off and hangs it on the coat hanger by the door. He then slips out of his boots, and I realize I still have mine on, having dripped water across the floor in my haste to light a fire. Finally, he wipes both hands from the front to the back of his head, his thick curls having transformed into tight coils. I pull my hair to one side and squeeze down the length, releasing the water into my hands, which I then wipe down my thighs, as if they're not also soaked.

When I look up, Junior has already crossed the room and is standing directly in front of me. His expression is unreadable as he holds my gaze. "Give me your foot," he eventually says.

"Huh?"

"You heard me. Give me your foot." He reaches down and hooks his hand behind my knee. I have to hold onto his shoulders to keep my balance when he draws my foot up toward him and begins pulling my boot off.

"I can't take my own damn boots off."

"Well, you didn't, and I don't want you tracking back toward the door again," he retorts, dropping the first foot and gesturing for me to give him the other one. I swallow and comply. Before he pulls this boot off, he tosses the other to where his are sitting. When he releases my leg again, his hand glides up my thigh to grasp onto my hip until I've caught my balance. A shiver runs down my spine, but I doubt it's from the cold this time. Instead, heat creeps up my body, following the trail of his hand.

"I-I caught a chill and was worried about getting a fire started," I manage to stammer out without looking up at him.

His hands sit on my shoulders, and I think he's going to shake me for my stubbornness. I'm surprised when his voice is softer. "You're soaked through. Let me get you a shirt to change into. We'll hang yours by the stove to dry before you catch cold." He walks toward the only other door in the room before turning back to me. "Thanks for getting the fire started." He steps into what I imagine must be his bedroom, and I hear him rummaging around. Light flickers in the room, and I find my feet moving in that direction before my brain catches up.

A small gasp leaves my throat when I catch sight of Junior. Thin pajama pants hang low on his hips, and he's pulling a tee over his head. His abs and chest are what sculptors aspire to create. *Fuck, he's delicious*, and suddenly, it's not only my clothes that are wet. He looks up and finds me staring. The smirk that takes over his face ignites a fire within me, and I know I'm in dangerous territory with this man.

Once his shirt is in place, he walks over and hands me another t-shirt. "Close the door. I don't know if I can just stand and watch."

Fuck me, I hope this storm lasts all damn night.

17

YOU TAKE MY CONTROL AWAY

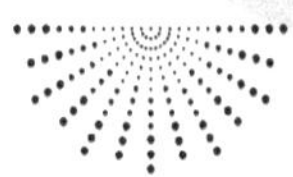

*J*unior

The door clicks behind me, and I let out a whoosh of air. The fact that I know she's undressing in my bedroom has my entire body on edge. I'll make something quick for dinner, something to busy my hands before I walk back in that room. I stoke the fire in the stove and check that the top plate is hot enough before setting a skillet on top of it. I'm in the process of patting out burgers when the bedroom door creaks open. Thankfully, I'm shaping the meat over the skillet because it falls out of my hands as my mouth drops open.

Joanna walks through the living space wearing nothing besides my t-shirt that barely comes to the tops of her thick thighs. There's no doubt that if she turns around, it will be stretched tightly across her ass, barely covering her cheeks. I don't know what I was expecting when I offered her the shirt, but this wasn't it. I wasn't prepared. Rather, my brain wasn't prepared, but my cock is definitely ready.

"Didn't I leave you pants too?" I manage to croak out, my mouth unsure what to do with itself.

Her cheeks tinge pink, and she looks down at the floor. "I couldn't fit them," she says so quietly, I almost don't hear her.

"What?"

The question comes out more incredulous than I intend, and I see the moment she becomes defensive. There's nothing to defend. She can parade around my house like that however and whenever she wants, but I will not be held accountable.

"All this ass wouldn't fit in your pants," she says, her chin raised in defiance, like she's daring me to say something else.

When she slaps her thighs in emphasis, making them jiggle, I fight to keep my eyes glued to hers. My breathing, however, gives me away, not to mention the drool that is likely dripping from my lips. Sizzling in the pan breaks whatever tether there is between our stares, and I look down to see where my nicely patted burger is browning into a log where it had fallen. *Dammit*, I say to myself. To her, I give a reassuring, "Wear whatever makes you comfortable," and set to trying to smash the burger back into shape.

She carries her jeans out to hang over the chair nearest to the stove. I try to keep my focus on the contents of the skillet, but she's turned around, giving me a perfect view of her juicy ass. Just as I thought, the shirt is stretching perfectly across the fullness of her, and my eyes follow her as she walks back toward the bedroom. She turns and looks at me. Caught. That's what I am. I'm caught up in her. A small smirk lifts her lip before she disappears into the room.

Fuck this. I grab the skillet off the stove and slide it onto the counter. After wiping my hands on the dishtowel, I follow her before I can change my mind.

I walk through the door to the most glorious sight possible. Joanna is bent over, picking up clothes from the floor...my clothes. "Leave them," I say, my voice deep and dark. A small gasp echoes through the room, and I wait for her to stand. I'm mesmerized by her, even as she shifts positions, dropping my jeans and shirt back onto the floor in a pile. I walk up behind her and run my fingers up her arms to her shoulders. Goosebumps spring up in the wake of my touch, and a shudder runs up her spine.

"Fancy, I...fuck!" I grab a handful of her hair and pull her head to the side, turning her until I can capture her lips with mine. She moans into my mouth, and that's all it takes for me to completely lose my grip on all the reasons I'm supposed to say no to this. There's no logic when her scent invades my senses, and I'm drowning in her sweet mouth. My hands explore, grab, caress, and pull her tighter against me.

She pulls on the drawstring of my pajama pants at the same time I grab the hem of the T-shirt she's wearing and start pulling it upward. We're in a tug of war to remove the barriers between our bodies. Finally, she lets me pull the shirt over her head, and she immediately drops to the floor, yanking my pants down with her. My cock damn near jumps into her waiting mouth, so hot and wet, and she moans around the thickness between her lips.

If I thought finding her bent over in nothing more than my shirt and a pair of panties was the sexiest sight, I was wrong. Nothing will ever compare to the view of her on her knees in front of me with my cock between her pouty lips. When her eyes lock on mine, the need to own her takes over. I grab her hair in both hands and begin rocking my hips. She reaches around and grabs my ass, fingers digging in to hold on tight while I fuck her mouth.

I watch her eyes for the slightest shift, but they remain determined and full of desire. She wants this as much as I do. That realization steals a moan from my throat, and the urge to come has my balls tightening. I pull her head back off of me, and strings of saliva run from the tip of my cock to her open mouth.

"Do you know how fucking beautiful you are right now? On your knees, your mouth swollen from sucking my cock. So fucking beautiful."

She continues to watch me, a smile spreading across her face as she reaches up and wipes the saliva across my tip and down my shaft. Her hand begins pumping my cock, slowly at first with long, tight strokes, and then she speeds up the movement.

"If I come now, we're both going to be sorely disappointed," I say, my voice hoarse.

"Says who?"

I grab her hand and reach down to pull her to stand in front of me. "Me. Now, kneel your pretty self on the edge of the bed." She looks like she wants to argue, but only for a second before she turns her back to me. Before she can even take her first step, I wrap my arm around her, pulling her flush to my body, my still-hard cock between us, my balls brushing against the top of her ass. "You're taking all of my self-control away, Fancy," I grind out, reaching up to cup her full tits. Her nipples are already puckered taut, and I pinch them until she moans, leaning back into me.

"I knew you were going to be trouble when I saw you walk into your own store. So damn beautiful and strong. Not just physically, but an inner strength that calls to me. So much fucking trouble." I run one of my hands down and into her panties, her soaked panties. This time, it's my moan that fills the room at the same moment I find her clit with the tip of my middle finger. I trail kisses across her shoulder, licking and sucking my way up her neck. I take her earlobe between my teeth, and she moans my name. "So much trouble," I say again before walking her forward until her legs are against the bed. "On your knees."

She complies immediately, and my cock twitches at the beautiful view of her ass up in the air. I pull the panties down her thighs, and her glistening pussy spreads open for me. I give myself a little rub, trying to calm the urge to plow into her. There's something else I need first. Spreading her open with my hands, I trail kisses between her cheeks and down around her lips. Her legs lean forward as if she might collapse onto the bed, and I slap her ass. "Don't run from me, Joanna."

18

NO RSVP NEEDED

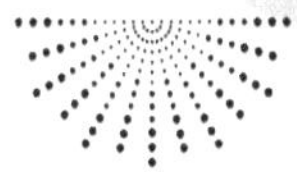

*J*oanna

The sound of my name in his husky voice and the sting of his hand on my ass are damn near my undoing. He calls me trouble, but I'm the one in danger. His hands and mouth are apt to wring orgasms from my body as easily as he's been able to worm his way into my every thought. I can't bring myself to say heart, but that is the danger. When body and mind align, the heart's not far behind.

When a second slap stings my other ass cheek, I cry out on a moan, and he chuckles from behind me. I want to admonish him, to yell that this is no laughing matter, but then he rubs the spot before running his fingers down between my lips and fully inserting two into my pussy. He slowly works them in and out, and I hear him drop to his knees, his breath blowing across my clit.

"Yes. Fuck," explodes from my mouth the moment his tongue touches my sensitive flesh. He swirls the tip around my nub and then sucks it into his mouth, all the while, his fingers fuck in and out of me faster.

"I want you to come for me. Come all over me. I want to taste every fucking drop."

His words. His voice. The stark difference between the professional he's always shown at the barn and the dominant lover he's become here, in this space. It all has me dripping, ready to do whatever he asks.

My hips buck, pushing his fingers deeper into me as I ride his face. My breathing is little more than pants and moans as every part of me strains to plunge from the precipice he's brought me to. He moans along with me, the sounds of a starving man getting the first taste of his favorite meal. It's more than I can take, and I shatter, my walls clenching as his intruding fingers wring pleasure from them with every wave. He continues to lick and suck, reaching his free arm around my legs to hold me still when all I want to do is collapse from the exertion.

When he finally slides his fingers out of me, a whimper leaves my lips without permission. The emptiness is overwhelming, and I don't know what to do with the emotions. They make no sense. Attraction, desire, lust, passion. Those all make sense. The loss of connection and subsequent sadness don't. I force myself to turn my head to look back at him, and he's there, staring at me with something akin to reverence on his face. His beautifully handsome face, damp with the remnants of my release. He finally shifts his gaze to mine, and our eyes lock.

"Do you have any fucking idea how goddamned good you taste? How beautiful you are?" His voice is low, like he's afraid loud sounds will shatter the moment when it's me already shattered. His touch, his expressions, his words. He has shattered me in a way no one else ever has before.

I turn over, scooting to the edge of the bed, my feet on either side of his legs, sliding up and down his thighs where he still kneels on the floor at my feet. His hands come up to caress my thighs, his thumbs rubbing higher. I lean down and grab his face with both hands, pulling him up for a kiss, and he wraps his arms around my waist, pulling me down to straddle his lap.

His cock is long and hard, sitting between us, teasing at my slit with each movement. I gasp at the feel of him, at the friction of our contact. "Junior." His name is a plea made between breaths in the seconds our lips part before crashing together again.

"Tell me what you need, Fancy." His voice is deliciously husky, and his breaths are heavy. His need is just as evident as mine, but here he is asking for what I want.

"The same thing you want, cowboy." I rock my hips back and forth, rubbing myself along his length until he groans out my name like a warning. All that does is egg me on, pushing me to drive him as wild as I feel.

He grabs my ass with a growl, digging his fingers into my flesh to the point I'm sure there will be marks in the morning, but I don't care. I want this. I want him. His mouth trails kisses down my jaw, and I tilt my head back, giving him access to my neck, my nipples grazing against his chest. A shudder rolls through me at the friction on the sensitive tips, similar to the friction still happening between my legs. I am nothing but a big ball of need at this point, and everything I need is in this man.

"Fuck, Fancy, I feel you coating my cock, and all I want is to slide into you."

"Then what the fuck are you waiting for? Do you want a formal invitation because dammit, I formally invite you to fuck me. No RSVP needed."

Another groan leaves his lips, but this one is tinged with a chuckle, his lip curling up at the end. "Will I get a thank you card in the mail later?"

Is he fucking for real? I'm losing my mind, and he's making a joke. I glare at him. "Cowboy, if I have to get myself off…" I don't get to finish my statement, as he somehow manages to stand from where he was kneeling with me still held in his hands. I squeak in surprise at his show of strength and dexterity, and a little at the fear of being dropped.

"I'm not fucking you on the floor, Joanna. My Fancy deserves to be in the bed."

While my heart leaps at his words, my body screams. The bed, the floor, the shower, against the side of his car, or bent over the counter. It doesn't fucking matter.

"I just need you inside me," is all I actually say as he lays me out on his bed and situates himself between my thighs.

Once again, he kisses me, my face, my neck, my chest, teasing my nipples with his tongue and teeth. I writhe beneath him, lifting my hips, trying to regain the friction from earlier. When he finally aligns his tip with my entrance, I sigh contentedly and relax to let him in. He slowly pushes forward, so achingly slow, like he's trying to savor each inch, and I'm going out of my mind. I grab his hips, my nails, short as they are, digging into his flesh, trying to pull him flush against me, wanting him buried to the hilt.

He chuckles. "Impatient much?"

I shoot daggers at him, and he smirks, lifting my right leg around his hip, and pushes fully inside me. My eyes widen, and my mouth drops open on a gasp. He's stolen my senses, and I am filled with him like there is no space left for me. The sudden realization that I won't be the same when this is over is almost more than I can take. I turn my face from his, afraid he'll see the turmoil in my eyes and stop. I don't want that either. I want this. Him. Even if it hurts later.

He pulls out until only the tip is inside, and then he plunges forward, filling me anew. He moans. "You feel so fucking good. So fucking perfect. Such a perfect fit." Again, working himself in and out of me as he peppers me with praise. I'm struck dumb. I can't form words. The feel of him consumes me, my need mounting with each thrust. The ebb and flow of his movement coaxing mewls of pleasure from my throat.

The sounds of our moans rise and combine, dancing through the small house on a crescendo until we're both repeating each other's names like a chant. Joanna. Junior. Joanna. Junior. When my release comes, he takes my cries into his mouth where they mix with his own. He collapses his full weight onto me, and I hold him tightly to my chest, emotions swirling.

Junior rolls us to our sides, kisses my forehead, and pulls me close, entwining our legs. The intimacy of that possessive moment is too much, and I feel the familiar burn behind my eyes. I've been married before, dammit. I've been with other men. I've never been held like this, like I'm precious and worth holding onto. Never before have I wanted to be kept. In fact, I came here to join the rodeo circuit because I didn't want to be tied to one place anymore. What the fuck am I doing here wanting to be held and treasured by this man, this beautiful cowboy?

Within minutes, his breaths soften into the cadence of sleep, his entire body relaxed. Mine, on the other hand, is taut, rigid with doubt, confusion, and longing, making the minutes feel like hours of torture. I slowly, silently untangled myself from him and make my way into his bathroom. After cleaning up, I peek outside to see the evening sky has cleared, and I throw back on my damp clothes, escaping to the crisp mountain air. I find Clementine tethered beside Junior's mount and quickly untie her, needing to run back to the safety of my own bed. The sudden urge to run home is overwhelming. My bed in the team house will have to do.

*J*unior

I wake with a start, adrenaline pumping. Something is wrong, but my exhausted brain can't quite make sense of the feeling. A quick glance around the room tells me nothing is out of place. My bathroom light is on, but it isn't unusual for me to fall into bed without shutting that off. Walking out into the living room, the odd feeling seems to grow exponentially.

"Oh fuck!" Memories flood into me the moment I see the skillet of uneaten burgers on the counter. I grab ahold of the bar stools that serve as chairs. Her scent invades my nostrils and threatens to swallow me whole. What the fuck did I do? Scratch that, I know exactly what I, what we, did. Visions of her in my shirt, on her knees before me, spread open on my bed. My stomach curls in on itself.

I run to the kitchen window. Clementine is gone but Apple is still there, still tethered, still wearing his saddle. The storm has ended outside, but it rages around me now. I had fallen asleep wrapped around her like a cloak, our legs entwined. Where has she gone? How did I sleep through it all? Most importantly, why did she leave?

My first instinct is to go after her, though I have no idea how long she's been gone. Nor do I know what I'll say when I bust into the barracks looking for her. Instead, I pace my living room trying to figure out what had gone wrong. No sooner do I flop into my chair without any answers than my phone buzzes.

Thinking it has to be Joanna, I immediately slide my finger across the screen without looking. The voice on the other end is definitely not Joanna.

"Reggie?" Taylor's voice penetrates through the disappointment.

"Yeah, I'm here. Sorry, I just woke up from a nap."

"Since when do you nap, old man?"

I laugh, trying to stay in the moment and not think about Joanna. "You call me old man when your man is what…"

"Don't you even!"

"Okay, okay," I say, holding up my hands in mock surrender, though I know she can't see them. "What's up?" I hold my breath for a moment hoping everything at home is good and she's just calling to chat, not to tell me something's wrong with Jordan.

"Have you seen Joanna?" My heart jumps to my throat. "We

usually chat with her Monday and Thursday evenings, but she hasn't been answering her phone."

Fuck, what do I say to that? I can't just tell Taylor I lost myself inside her boyfriend's daughter and then the woman ran off when I fell asleep. If Garrett Daniels didn't already look at me like he wanted to choke the life out of me for hugging Taylor, he'd rip my head off for that.

"I saw her earlier. We had a pretty big storm up here, and she was out on the trails. I don't know that she took her phone."

"Is she okay? Does she know those trails?"

"She's fine. She's fine. I found her before the storm got bad, and we sheltered together until it was over. I never heard a phone ring, which is why I assume she didn't have it with her. Maybe she, like me, decided to take a nap once she took care of the horse upon returning to the barn after the storm."

The guilt for my lies of omission is nothing compared to the guilt I feel at not knowing if any of my speculation is true. Did she make it back to the barn safely? Was she able to get some sleep? Is she okay?

"I was just about to go back toward that end of the ranch to get some supper. If I see her, I'll tell her to give y'all a call, else I'll tell her in the morning. Does that work?"

I stand and start pulling on my jeans and a henley, opting for quick and easy. I need to check on her, even if it's just to know she hates me for what happened between us. My stomach clenches at the thought.

Taylor's voice once again breaks into my thoughts. "That sounds good. Her dad was disappointed, and his disappointment quickly turns into worry, which turns into me having to talk him out of hopping in the car and driving out there."

"Yeah, I don't think she'd want that." *And neither do I.* I keep that last thought to myself. "I'll make sure she calls y'all back, if nothing else to check in by mid-morning tomorrow."

"Thanks!"

We hang up, and I pull on my boots before heading out the door. Apple whinnies at me, and I apologize for leaving him like a pack mule for so many hours. Then we make our way back down to the barn. Though it's later than I originally thought, I need to see her, even if she doesn't want to see me.

RUNNING SCARED

Joanna

I race into the barn on Clementine's back. I'm not sure of the exact time or how long I'd spent in Junior's cabin, but it's already dark outside. Hopefully, that means everyone else will either be home with their families or in the barracks. I should've known better, though. In the month I've been here, there's always been someone awake and moving about in the barn. I've just always assumed it was Junior working way into the night. Tonight, however, I know for sure it's not him.

Jerry comes from around the corner with a small box in his hand as I lead Clementine into her stall, preparing to rub her down and feed her after all she's done for me today. I jump, startled to see him slinking around from the dimly lit area.

"Jesus, Jerry, you scared the shit out of me."

His eyes sparkle, but I get the sense that gleam is not mirthful. Instead, he looks irritated to find me here.

"I can take care of that for you," he offers, a smile flashing across his face.

Unease settles into my chest. "I got it, thanks. What's in the box?"

He looks down as if he'd forgotten he's carrying it. His smile falters, and he takes two steps toward the stall. "C'mon, I know you missed dinner. Let me take care of her for you."

"No, really. I worked her. I'll take care of her. You should get some rest." Something about his insistence makes me even more reluctant to release her to him. I barely know him since he was out of commission for my first two weeks here, and the fact that she had kicked him tells me she'd probably rather anyone care for her but him. "So, what's that?" I ask when he doesn't move. I look pointedly at the box in his hand, hoping that asking about it again will get him to leave.

"This? Oh, nothing," he says with a sheepish grin. Something in his expression, though, says that the grin is a facade. There's definitely something else going on with him, and I don't like it.

"Oh well, like you said, it's late, and I do need some rest, so I'm gonna go take care of Clementine now. You have a good night." I don't have the bandwidth to parse through Jerry's behavior and his obvious lies when my mind and body are screaming about Junior. Clementine and I head toward her stall, and Jerry must get the hint because he finally turns on his heel and leaves out the side door.

"That was so weird," I whisper to Clementine, and she sighs. "Yep, I'm glad he's gone too."

*J*oanna

Thirty minutes later, Morgan's voice lifts in concern and yet holds a twinge of huskiness that means she was either on the verge or had been completely asleep. "J? Is everything alright?"

"Of course," I respond, trying to keep my voice as upbeat as possible. "I can't call my best friend?"

Shuffling around is followed by the soft click of a door closing on the other end of the phone. It's a few more seconds before Morgan finally says, "Yes, of course, you can, but you don't. You haven't. And you damn sure wouldn't 'call your best friend' at this hour if everything was alright."

I can hear the implied air quotes and can't stifle a small chuckle. Only Morgan would be able to make me laugh when it feels like the world is caving in. "I've missed you."

"We all miss you, J. Now tell me what's going on."

"I think I may have fucked up. Like, I might need to come home early fucked up. You know Jordan's brother, right?"

"The hottie who came to the New Year's Eve party? Your new boss?"

"Yeah," I say, blowing out a big breath of air. Always so good at waiting, Morgan says nothing. "Well, he kissed me outside on Pa's porch."

"Do what now? And you're just now telling me this?"

"Well, I kinda kissed him too. I mean, it was a simple peck, yet it wasn't, you know? We were under the mistletoe, and it just sorta happened."

"Well damn!"

"Just hold that thought because it gets worse. Neither of us talked about it on the way to the ranch, just pretended like it didn't happen. For a couple weeks, we just ignored it. Then we went into town to put up flyers for a small exhibition they're having here at the ranch the end of the month, and well…"

"Well, what?? Damn, don't leave me in suspense." Her voice has risen, and she gasps before going back to a whisper. "Don't make me wake the guests, or worse, your brother."

I snort. "Well, Junior's really funny, and sweet, and down-to-earth, and…"

"And?" Again, her voice rises with the question.

"And hotter than sin. Morgan, he kissed me again outside the library, and I had my legs around his waist before I could think straight. If someone else wouldn't have slammed their car door, we might've fucked right in the parking lot in front of God and all of Main Street."

"Whoa!"

Yeah, whoa is what I thought too, but it didn't stop me from wanting to ride him like a horse. I don't say that part out loud. She won't judge me, but some things are just better kept inside.

"So, what happened?"

"We went back to the ranch. Obviously, we couldn't be trusted alone together, even in public. That was two weeks ago."

"Two weeks ago?" She pauses her question, as if waiting for further explanation, but the words freeze in my throat. "You didn't call me this late tonight because of something that happened two weeks ago."

I stand up from my bed and begin pacing in my small room. "No, I didn't call you about two weeks ago." I drop my voice as if someone might be eavesdropping. It's not like I haven't already said enough to cause Junior and I trouble, but this is far more than a chaste Christmas kiss or a moment of weakness in a parking lot. "We holed up in his cabin during a storm." Though Morgan says nothing, I can picture her waiting with bated breath. "Is there such a thing as cowboy magic?" I ask, my voice sounding breathier than intended. Morgan giggles on the other end. "Seriously, he wove some kind of spell around me, and before I knew it, I was on my knees with him in my mouth."

Morgan gasps. "Damn, girl. That's hot! So, what's the problem?"

"You mean beside him being my boss?" I sit on the edge of my bed and rest my chin on my hand. "I really like him."

"Okay..." she draws out.

"No, I mean, I really like him. Coming together with him was like something I'd never experienced before, like a melding of sorts. That sounds crazy, right? We've barely known each other a month."

"And you kissed him just a couple days after meeting," she

reminds me. "So, it's not like there wasn't some kind of attraction or chemistry there to begin with."

"I can't do this, Morgan. I left Cole County because I wanted to be free of ties for a while. I didn't leave to make a connection like this in the first place I landed."

"I see now."

I wait a few moments for her to explain what she means. My anxiety about the whole situation is already on ten, and the silence is grating. "What do you see, oh Great Morgana?"

"Just because you're scared, don't get pissy with me, J."

"Scare...scared? I'm not scared."

"You are. You felt trapped here, and you're afraid that if you fall for the guy, you'll be trapped there. But maybe you only felt trapped because you felt stuck and lonely while everyone else was finding their way forward. I can see how that could be true, and I hate that for you because we all love you. I just know from experience, it's not the same."

"You know, I hate you sometimes," I say quietly around the knot in my throat.

"That thin line is a bitch," she responds, and a chuckle escapes my lips.

I flop back on the bed. "I'm sorry for waking you. Please don't tell Jacob or Taylor. I definitely don't want Pa to know."

"You'll figure it out, J. You're one of the most level-headed people I know. If you have feelings for that man, it's because you recognize a man worthy of your feelings, not for any other reason."

Letting out a sigh, I tell her goodnight and let my mind replay her words. Am I just scared? Could it really be that simple? I immediately knew that messing with Junior Thompson would be like playing with fire, but I had only thought of it in terms of my job, not the chance of losing my heart. At some point, I drift off to sleep feeling guilty about the way I left his cabin without a word or a note. I'll eventually owe him an apology.

THERE YOU ARE

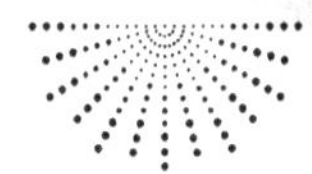

*J*unior

The barn is almost completely dark when I walk Apple through the gate. Of course, the first place my eyes go is to the door of Clementine's stall. It's thankfully closed, and I can see the horse's head just over the edge. That means Joanna made it back here, at least.

I thought maybe I'd be able to catch her at supper, but the kitchen is already closed and cleaned up by now. Not gonna lie, I had thought Taylor's call was a little dramatic until I realized that it was already nearly 9pm, which means it was ten in Colliers Town. Considering we all get up super early for our jobs, I can see why she was worried.

As we approach Apple's stall, Jerry, one of the grooms, comes around the corner out of the shadows. "What the hell, Jer!"

The kid jumps like he was the one caught off guard and not me. "Junior. Damn man, sorry. I didn't know you were in here."

"What the hell are you doing here at this hour?"

He looks at me, and there's guilt in his eyes, but he quickly shakes it away. I can only imagine he probably had a tryst with one of the young female riders or something like that. I can't blame him for a little late-night dalliance when the only reason I'm here at this hour is because I'd had one of my own earlier. An image of Joanna kneeling on my bed has me smiling before I see the kid's expression shift in confusion.

"Never mind. Do me a favor and take care of Apple before you head off to bed."

"Sure thing, boss." He visibly swallows before following up with a quick, "You have a good night."

I raise my hand in a wave as I head out in the direction of what we call the barracks, the building that houses the hands, grooms, riders, and travel vets. That's where Joanna's assigned to stay. Thankfully, Kelly's so meticulous in her documentation that I know exactly which room everyone is in and don't have to go fumbling around the building this late.

I lightly knock on the door, hoping I can keep from anyone else coming to check. When she doesn't answer, I knock a little harder. A groan comes from behind the door with a tired "what?" before the sound of feet approaches the door. It opens a crack, and her sleepy face comes into view a moment before her eyes go wide.

"Junior?" Her voice is a surprised whisper.

"Hey," I say quietly. "Can we talk for a minute?" I hold my breath, not sure if she'll let me in or tell me to go fuck myself. "Please."

A few painful moments pass before she takes a deep breath and opens the door enough for me to step inside. Nearly all the rooms in this building are the same. A twin bed sits against the wall, along with a small dresser and mirror. Everything else is dependent on the person. Many of our regulars decorate like they're staying in a college dorm, while others have pictures from home and maybe a chair or two. Joanna's room is stark, like she has no intention of staying for long. There's literally nothing of her in the room, and yet she fills it completely.

"What do you want to talk about?" Her voice is stiff, but

there's a crack at the end that captures my attention, especially when she hasn't looked directly at me since inviting me inside.

I stay silent, hoping she'll turn her eyes my way, until I can't take it anymore. "Joanna, look at me." I put a little force behind the words, and her eyes snap up to me. "There you are," I say much more softly. A hint of pink tints her cheeks, and she starts to look away. I run my hand along her jaw, pulling her face back towards me. "You already left me once tonight. Stay with me now."

"I'm sorry about that," she says, finally raising her gaze to meet mine. "I needed to get Clementine back and get to bed." She shifts with the last part, and I know she's lying.

"Is that really why you snuck off?"

She stiffens for a split second, like she wants to hold onto the lie, but then she relaxes. "No, not really. I needed to process everything. I needed to talk to someone."

"You can talk to me."

A loud "Ha!" leaves her lips at my words, and my face falls. It's like she's slapped me. Then she's shaking her head. "I couldn't talk to you about you, about this thing between us. If we were going to talk about that, it probably should've happened before tonight."

"You're right," I agree and sit on the corner of her bed. "I'm sorry."

"For what, Cowboy? For following the trail we've been blazing for weeks?"

"For whatever it was that chased you off."

"Me. It was all me. I'm a 36-year-old woman who's never before left her hometown. This was supposed to be an escape from the obligations that kept me trapped in Colliers Town all that time. All the fucking expectations that felt like weights on my shoulders every damn day..." She trails off, and her expression is pained, like she doesn't want to say the next part.

"It's okay. You can say it," I say, trying to reassure her.

"I wanted to travel. I took this job to travel the circuit and try and find what I'd been missing." My gaze drops to the floor. I can see where this is going, and I don't want to go there, but I promised to listen. Taking a deep breath, I prepare myself for the gut check. "I wasn't looking for someone to get involved with." She grabs my face in her hands, and squats in front of me. "That wasn't what I came here for, but it's what I've found, and it scares me."

I stare into her eyes for a few silent moments that might have been hours. I could drown in the honest depths of her ocean blue eyes. "You're right about one thing, Fancy." She sits back on her heels with an uncertain look on her face. I lean forward with a smile and kiss the tip of her nose. I just can't help myself. "What happened between us was most definitely inevitable."

She smiles back up at me. "Now what?"

Her question is loaded, and I wish I had an answer. "I'm not sure, honestly. It's probably not a good idea for it to go any further, considering I'm your boss." Her shoulders droop just a bit before she recovers and holds her head up. I grab her hands and pull them up to sit on my knees, so she's kneeling in front of me again. "It's probably not a good idea, but I've never been a rule follower. If I were, I'd likely still be near home and a doctor like my parents had wanted. Instead, I go after what I want and make a way."

"What exactly does that mean?" she asks with an uncomfortable chuckle.

She's looked down to where her hands lay on my knees, and I lift her chin with my fingers. "It means, I want to see where this goes, even if we keep it just between us. That is, if you're willing to break the rules with me."

WE DID THIS!

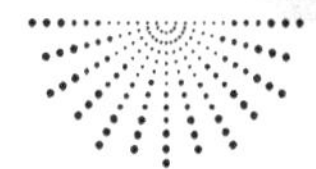

Joanna

As the exhibition date approaches, the barn is in a flurry of excitement and activity. The rental stands have to be set up, and the arena needs cleaned and prepped. The corrals need to be reinforced because the practice ones used for the broncs and bulls is on the other end of the ranch. When I ask about the previous showcases, Kelly enjoys recounting the very first one when one of the bulls not only knocked the fence down but chased Junior around for fifteen minutes before getting tired. My heart spent the full fifteen minutes of her story in my throat. While I know he's fine now, that knowledge doesn't help me feel any better about his near trampling and impromptu role of circus clown.

"Thankfully, there weren't many spectators for that one, huh?" I say, trying to distract from my obvious discomfort.

"Yeah," she concedes. "We learned a lot that year, and it's only gotten better since. Fingers crossed, this is going to be the best year yet!"

I smile at her enthusiasm, turning my face away to keep her from stopping. The woman is too damn somber most of the time.

Don't get me wrong, she's a pistol, and I occasionally hear the verbal sparring between her and Junior when I'm assigned one of the horses closest to his office, but she could probably give my curmudgeonly old man a run for his money.

My smile deepens when I think of how much he's changed this past year. Between Morgan and Taylor, they've pretty much brought Pa back to life, or rather, they've breathed new life into him, especially Taylor. *Gosh, I miss them all*, I think, and my eyes immediately start to sting. Quickly, I turn back to Kelly.

"So, why aren't we just hosting a rodeo? There's plenty of space, and I'm sure it'll be a hit."

Her eyes dull and then harden. "Damn Doughertys," she says without further explanation. I want to push for more information, but she turns away and heads out of the barn. I'll have to pry it from Junior. It's not like he's been very forthcoming about why their little exhibition had been so small in the first place, but knowing it has something to do with the ranch owners might give me some leverage to get the details from him.

Speaking of the man, even when it's only in my head, is like that cowboy magic I asked Morgan about a couple weeks ago because he's suddenly behind me. His arms encircle my waist, and his lips find my neck. When they make it up to my ear, he whispers a sensual hello.

"Just the man I wanted to see," I say and turn in his arms. There's hunger in his eyes, but I don't let that look, or what it does to my nether regions, deter me. "I was talking to Kelly about how, with all this land, animals, and awesome trainers, this place doesn't host its own rodeo." His eyes narrow, and I know he wants to call me out for putting it on thick, but I just give him a coy smile.

"Woman, there is nothing innocent about you."

"I have no idea what you mean. I was simply making an observation about how similarly built this ranch is to Boulder Ranch and how you could really put on a helluva show for more than just the locals." I let my brows draw together. "I was simply asking why you all hadn't thought of it yet." When he opens his mouth, I play my trump card. "She simply scoffed and said something like 'Fucking Doughertys.'"

Junior shakes his head. "It's not time yet is all. We're building."

I purse my lips and tilt my head just enough to let him know I see him dodging the question. There will be time to continue this conversation later, I tell myself. No need to push today when there's still so much to be done for the exhibition.

"What else is on the to-do list for the exhibition?"

"All the rental equipment should be here tomorrow. I just sent the final flyers to be printed, so those will have to be put up. Kelly is updating the logistics to include the additional teams and additional seating for spectators." He looks at me intently. "I'm hoping you're right about the numbers. We've ordered two extra sets of metal bleachers and invited two additional food trucks."

I pat his chest. "When do you want to go put up those flyers?" I ask, stepping back and picking up my rake. There are still more stalls to be mucked and horses to be exercised before the day ends. Junior grabs my hand and pushes me against the wall, his other hand at my hip. A small gasp leaves my lips as I lean into him, and he presses his lips to mine, deftly sliding his tongue inside my parted lips. Letting the rake fall to the floor, I reach around to dig my fingers into his ass and pull him tight against me. He moans into my mouth, and I grind myself against him. All thoughts of being discreet and the myriad of reasons why we shouldn't be doing this fade away at the glorious feel of him.

"Junior," I say, finally trying to push back from his embrace. "I have work to do, and my boss is difficult."

"Your boss," he says after wiping his mouth, "won't interfere, if he knows what's good for him." He takes a couple breaths, his eyes never leaving mine. "About those flyers..." I raise a brow but remain silent. "I think we need to, um, take care of those this evening. We can eat while we're in town."

"Will we actually eat, or will it end up like those burgers we were supposed to have last time?" I know I shouldn't be teasing him. I know I should be keeping my distance and trying to keep things professional. Then he touches me, and I forget it all.

He leans in close to my ear. "I'll make sure you're well fed. You'll need your energy."

Clean up on Aisle five! Someone bring a firehose and a new pair of panties. I open my mouth to say something, to give some kind of retort, but no sound comes out. Junior chuckles low in his throat and kisses my neck before pulling away and leaving the barn.

Clementine whinnies from her stall. "I know what you mean, girl," I respond while retrieving my rake and getting back to work.

*J*unior

I should've been prepared for it after the past couple years, but tensions have been crazy high all week as we put in the final preparations for this weekend's showcase. Last night, two of our riders got into a fight right after we'd posted the order of events. This morning, one of the field hands nearly got his head knocked off by Kelly when he started yelling about the way we've cordoned off the back lot for parking. I had to step in to save his life.

The one thing that's kept me grounded is Joanna's excitement about the event. She's stepped in to help wherever needed. She directed the bleacher assembly and placements, and she ensured all the food trucks were set up in a way that was safe and made sense. It's like she has a natural eye for event planning. Every time something has gone off the rocker, I look for her. Most of the time, she doesn't even notice me watching, but her steady presence comforts me. This expanded event will either be our next step toward a rodeo of our own or the nail in the coffin. Neither Jack nor Lawson will let me get away with public failure when they really didn't want anyone here in the first place.

"Stop worrying," Kells says from my side before I realize she's standing there.

"You were ready to send that kid to the hospital, and you're telling me not to worry?"

She lets out a sly chuckle, but I know it's a front. I could see the guilt written all over her face this morning when I finally stepped between them. She's tough, and she runs a tight ship in the barns, but she's not an asshole either.

"Did you see the line at the ticket booth?" she asks when silence stretches between us. "What about the line of cars waiting to park still?" Her elbow nudges mine arm. "It's going to be great! You've outdone yourself this time, boss."

I turn to face her. "I sure as fuck hope so, Kells. This needs to blow everyone away, or they'll likely shut down the entire thing."

Her face hardens in a fierceness I've rarely seen. "Then I guess we better get out of this barn and go make sure everything goes as planned."

With a nod, I hold out my fist, and she bumps hers against mine. We walk out into the open air and head in opposite directions. "Let's do this!" I say under my breath.

22

PUNISHMENT IT IS

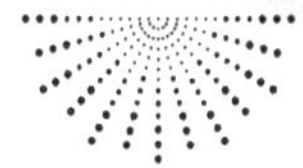

*J*unior

The crew piles into my office. There's hardly enough room for everyone to stand let alone find seats. Kelly passes cups around. "To our leader," she says, lifting her cup in my direction. I nod in acknowledgement. She knows I'm not a big fan of public praise. We are a team. "This event was Junior's brainchild five years ago, and it has grown each year thanks to his leadership. This year, however, was something truly amazing. Not only did we have more visitors to the ranch, but there were more out-of-towners, and the riders got the recognition they're due for their hard work at each and every event." Her eyes glisten when she looks in my direction again.

I lift my cup back in her direction. "I could not have done any of this without all of you. Your trust, your dedication, and your belief in our team and this event are what keep it going each year. This year, I have to add an additional bit of gratitude to our newest member."

My eyes catch Joanna's, and she shakes her head. We've not spent more than a few stolen moments together since the other night when we put up the final flyers. That Thursday in her room, after she left my cabin, we had agreed to keep things simple and as casual as possible. We acknowledged that the attraction was too strong to just try and beat down like it wasn't there but that we wouldn't let it cause havoc in our lives and work, at least not until we get to know each other better and decide it's worth putting everything on the line to move forward. That last part may have been more of her doing than mine, but I can respect it. She's trying to protect my job and reputation while also allowing herself the opportunity to enjoy the freedom away from Cole County. Still, I ache to have her next to me, even in this room full of people.

"Joanna gave me the idea to expand our marketing efforts and to add in the other family-friendly activities, including the meet and greet that was such a hit. The growth of this year's event is in large part thanks to her suggestions." I lift my cup in her direction and take the shot. Everyone else gives a hardy shout of 'Cheers' before downing their own shots and filing out of the room.

When it's just Joanna, Kelly, and me in the room, Kelly congratulates us both. "Great teamwork, you two! I know the owners aren't yet ready for us to put on anything more than an exhibition, but I hope today's success is just one more chink in the armor they've put up around this place. Our horses and riders are top notch, and that's not even counting the work happening with our bull riders and ropers." She pours us each another shot.

"One day, Kells. One day."

She takes my words as a toast to the future and lifts her glass, downing the tequila without even the slightest wince. Joanna and I follow her lead. Kelly sets the near-empty bottle on my desk and walks out of the office, pulling the door closed behind her.

"Today was truly amazing, Cowboy. You did well."

"We did well," I correct her. "I meant what I said about today's success being, in large part, because of you telling me to think bigger."

She blushes, and it sparks a fire in the middle of my chest. Of course, her blush and my heat could be a result of the tequila, but I doubt it. I can't take my eyes off her.

"Now that the exhibition is over, we'll be taking this show on the road. Are you ready to ride, Fancy?" I drop my voice an octave when I ask the last question.

A smile threatens at the corners of her mouth. Rather than respond immediately, though, she pours the remainder of the bottle into our two cups and passes me mine. "Are you asking whether I'm packed for traveling with the team, or whether I think I can last eight seconds."

"Oh, you got a lot of try in you, Fancy. I have no doubt you can cover, but the ride would be so worth it." Her face flushes again, and a smile tugs at my lips when I take the shot. "I know we said we'd keep this thing between us cool, but I'd be lying if I said seeing you blush doesn't make my damn cock hard."

"Is that so?"

"Come around here, and I'll show you."

She turns away from me and walks toward the door without a backward glance. I close my eyes against the tightening in my chest, the ache there nearly as painful as the one in my cock. Rather than hear the door open and close, a click of the lock rings through the office. My head snaps up to see her sauntering my way. I suck in a breath at the desire simmering in her beautiful eyes. When she gets to the side of my desk, I go to stand, reaching for her, but she pushes me back onto my chair.

"Just sit there and behave yourself, Cowboy. You can do that, right?"

I hold back the smirk threatening to take over my face. She pulls her shirt over her head, the lace bra showing everything, and my mouth waters. I bite the inside of my cheek to keep from reaching out. I'm in agony holding myself back, but curiosity has me sitting on my hands. She unbuttons the fly of her jeans and peels them off, watching me the whole time. I can't hold back the groan when my cock swells beyond what's comfortable.

"Joanna. Fancy, I..." My voice is little more than a whisper when she puts a finger to my lips. I growl in protest and nip at the tip.

She slaps at my chest and chuckles. "Is that what you call behaving?"

"That depends," I drawl. "Are you gonna punish me?" Her eyes sparkle with mischief. "Punishment it is, then. Do your worst, Fancy."

*J*oanna

Something about Junior telling me to punish him has me tingling all over. I quickly look about the office until my eyes land on the rope and whip hanging on the wall by his bathroom door. I give him a sly smile.

"Close your eyes, Cowboy, and I may go easy on you."

He gives a low chuckle but then does as I say. I grab the items and bind his arms to the chair. When he starts protesting, I threaten to put my clothes back on and leave. Unsurprisingly, he settles back into the seat and keeps his eyes closed. Once I have both hands held in place, I move his keyboard and papers out of the way and sit my ass up on the edge of the desk, resting my feet on his knees. He spreads his legs, taking mine with them, but he still doesn't open his eyes.

"Look at you listening so well." I wrap the whip around my neck twice, so the handle and the tip both hang over my breasts. Stretching my leg out a bit, I rub my toes over the bulge in his jeans. He hisses, and I smile. "You seem to be wound a little tight there."

Though his eyes are closed, he draws his brows together in a scowl, making me laugh. "Let me show you what wound up looks like," he offers, his voice husky. I think back to that day in his cabin where he had wound me up with his tongue and fingers before fucking me breathless. As much as I want a repeat of that afternoon, I want to hear him begging first.

"Tell me what you want, Cowboy. What do you want to do to me? This," I say while rubbing against his jeans again, "says that you have a naughty mind."

"You have no idea."

"Then use your words."

"I'd rather use what you're rubbing against."

His nostrils flare, and I can tell he's struggling to keep himself in check. It's not like I tied him so tight he couldn't get loose if he wanted to. He's staying put for my benefit.

"Play nice, and I may just let you. Else, I'll have to do it all myself." I trail my hands down over my breasts, squeezing my nipples through my bra. My eyes roll at the sensation. There's no way I'll last long playing this game with him. "If I untied you, what would you do to me." I slide my hand into my panties, already wet with my need for him. A gasp escapes my lips when my fingers touch my clit.

A smile slides across his lips. "What're you doing, Fancy?"

Fighting to control my breathing and my voice, I answer him with as much nonchalance as I can muster. "I'm waiting for you to follow directions."

He chuckles. "So, if I open my eyes, I won't see you touching yourself?"

"If you open your eyes without doing what I asked, you won't see anything besides me leaving."

"What I want to do right now is pull you over my lap and spank you. I want to mark you with my handprint." I bite my lip to keep from moaning at the thought, and I begin to work my clit again. "Then, when I know you're dripping, I'm going to finger both your holes until you scream my name. You do know my real name, don't you, Fancy?"

"Reggie," I breathe out.

"That's it, baby. You like to picture my hands all over you, my mouth on you, don't you?"

"Yes."

"Let me watch you."

I pull my tits from my bra and run the tip of the whip over my nipples, moaning at the sensation.

"Joanna." My name is a plea.

I take the whip handle and rub it down across my panties, pressing hard enough to tease my clit, already sensitive from my fingers. An even louder moan leaves my lips.

"Fuck, please." When he gets no response from me, other than my heavy breathing, he begs. "Baby, if you won't let me watch, then finger yourself and let me hear it. I need to know how wet you are for me."

My breath hitches, and I barely get the words out giving him permission to open his eyes. His gaze travels up from where my toes are perched on his knees to where I've slid the handle of the whip into my panties, the texture still rubbing my clit in the most delicious way. The way his eyes take me in, I nearly come undone. Pulling my bottom lip between my teeth, I bite down so hard, surprised I don't taste blood. By the time his gaze reaches my face, taking in the whip wrapped around my throat, he's panting. Using his legs for leverage, I lift my ass and slide my panties off and down my thighs. He leans forward and grabs them with his teeth when I go to toe them off my ankles.

"Did I give you permission to taste my panties?" I ask with a smirk.

He shakes his head. "You also didn't stop me."

"So hardheaded."

"It's not just the head that's hard right now."

After a few seconds of watching my face, his gaze is drawn back down my body to where I'm now dipping the handle into my wetness. It's not enough to fuck myself or to get me off, but enough for him to see and hear how fucking wet I am.

"Fuck, Joanna, don't make me come in my pants like a teenager. You look so fucking sexy using my whip as a dildo, but you know it would feel much better with my cock going in and out of you."

I pull on the tip of the whip, holding it tight against my nipple while I pull the handle back down to my entrance. When it tightens around my throat with the tiniest amount of pressure, I gasp, and spasms of pure pleasure take over my body. His eyes jump to mine, holding my gaze.

"Oh my, fuck." I gasp out.

He relaxes against the back of the chair, his breaths erratic. "That was. Fuck, baby, that was the sexiest thing I think I've ever seen."

"Lick me clean," I say once I'm finally able to form words.

A single brow raises, and he slides his hands out of the rope. Before I can protest, he buries his face in my pussy, lapping me from back to front, dipping his tongue inside of me. He doesn't move on until he coaxes a moan from my lips.

"I didn't say fuck me with your tongue, Cowboy."

"Tell me to stop then."

Neither of us say another word, and within minutes, he has me coming again all over his face. The barn is dark and quiet by the time we leave his office, both of us sated.

"We'll be heading south next week for a couple of exhibitions before making our way to Cole County for the Boulder Ranch opening ceremony," he says as he walks me to the barracks. "You never did answer my question about being ready."

I don't know what to say. I'm ready to travel. I'm ready to stay close to him. I'm ready to see my family again after all this time. But am I ready for my time to be up? Am I ready to go home? I don't know.

"I will be," is all I manage to say before he heads back to his cabin.

23

WATCHING FROM THE SHADOWS

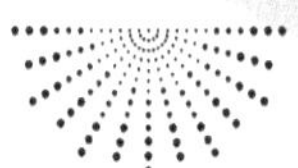

Junior

The pre-season exhibition circuit is always a crapshoot. Many of the teams send in untried riders for each of the events, so we don't always know what we're up against. Every time the announcer says an unfamiliar name, we all hold our breaths. There are many positives too, though. Our team gets more trial runs to care for the animals and try new riding techniques before the points start counting. Most of our riders have already started racking up wins and building morale, and Joanna has proven herself to be an awesome cheerleader. She even gives pep talks to those who've lost their events, and they leave the arena with smiles on their faces.

I watch her rubbing down Clementine after the barrel races are over. There's such a peaceful look on her face whenever she's near that horse. Chloe, Clementine's rider since last year, has greatly improved since last season, but the real change has been with Clementine herself. She has been at the top of her game ever since Joanna became her primary handler. There's a chemistry between them, something that wasn't there with Jerry.

Joanna looks up and locks eyes with me. I want to pretend I

haven't been watching her but can't bring myself to look away. Whenever she's in the vicinity, my eyes naturally drift to her like a magnet. My fingers itch to run through her hair the same way she's running hers through Clementine's main. What my body wants to do afterwards is less wholesome, though somehow more intimate.

Memories of her on my desk pleasuring herself with my whip flash through my mind, and I have to take a few awkward steps to adjust the way my dick sits in my jeans. I can barely think her name without getting hard nowadays. The more time I spend with her, and the more memories I have of her in every position, the worse it gets. It's like my cock seeks her out. Unfortunately, we haven't been anywhere long enough these past couple weeks for me to get her alone.

Soon, we'll be back in Cole County for the opening ceremony at Boulder Ranch, and I'll get some time with her. I have to. It may be my last chance. It's time for her to decide if she's going to continue on with us or...I don't even want to continue that train of thought. Instead, I follow her out to Clementine's trailer to sneak up behind her.

I stop in my tracks before I get there, though. Someone is lurking between the horse trailers. Anger spikes. Who the fuck would be hanging out between our trailers? I watch them round Clementine's trailer at the same time Joanna and Clementine come around the barn. A wave of protectiveness surges through me, and I quickly and quietly make my way around the trailer. Whoever the person is, they're standing there watching Joanna with Clementine. They've not said a word or announced their presence. Though the silhouette looks familiar, I can't quite make out who the person is from this position.

"Hey there! What're you doing?" I say once I'm close enough to make myself known without spooking the horses. The person stiffens, but they don't turn around. "Who are you, and why are you by my trailers?" A bucket hits the ground, grabbing both of our attention. Mine is pulled to the sliver of Joanna's face I can see between the trailer body and the door. It's enough of a distraction for the person to take off running. My fists clench, and I take a deep breath to keep from growling in frustration. Hopefully, it was just a kid trying to get up close and personal with the horses and riders.

*J*oanna

"Your steps are too heavy to be trying to sneak around, Junior Thompson," I say without turning my head.

His arms snake around my waist and pull me back against him as I close and lock the trailer door, securing Clementine inside for the night. I lean back against his chest, my head barely reaching his shoulder, and he trails kisses from my temple down to my neck, gently nipping at the skin where my neck and shoulder meet.

It's only been a couple weeks since our last bit of alone time in his office, but it feels like months. Every time I feel him watching me, my body yearns for his touch, but there are always too many people around. This is the first time he's approached me since we left the ranch, and I'm desperate for more. Turning in his arms, I pull his mouth to mine, ready to climb him like a tree right here and now. He pushes me back against the trailer, and I moan, wrapping my legs around him when he reaches down and grabs my ass with both hands.

"Look at you, so hot for me. It seems like you've missed me, Fancy," he rasps out between kisses. "I bet if I slid my hand into those painted on jeans, you'd be soaked."

I begin rocking my hips, rubbing my core against the hardness in his jeans before responding. "I bet if I do this long enough, your pants will be wet too."

We both laugh, and he puts me back on the ground.

He kisses the tip of my nose just as they announce the last event. He turns to leave but then stops, and a serious look takes over his face. "Hey, you didn't happen to see anyone lurking around the horses or the trailers since we've been here, have you?"

"When? Today?" My brows knit together.

"Yeah." He doesn't say anything more for a moment, his eyes staring off into the distance, around the back of the barn. "As I was sneaking up on you..." His gaze lands on me as I try to hold in my response at the idea he could have possibly snuck up on anyone. "Don't you dare laugh, Fancy! I would've succeeded if I hadn't gotten distracted by someone else hiding in the shadows between the trailers."

A shudder runs up my spine. "There was someone here? What were they doing? Are they still around? Did you see who it was?"

His hands grab my upper arms, rubbing up and down to calm me. "Don't worry. They're not here now. I snuck up and scared them off," he says with a raised brow, and I playful swat at his chest. "It was probably an overenthusiastic fan or a teenage hopeful who wanted to see what the horses looked like up close."

I search his face, unsure if his speculation is for my benefit or something he truly believes. Something isn't sitting right with me just like it hadn't that day in the barn when I'd run into Jerry. We don't just run into people around our horses. "No," I say. "The only incident that even comes close was a couple months ago back at the ranch. That day we got caught up in the cabin, Jerry scared the shit out of me by coming out of the shadows in the barn." He looks at me intently, waiting for me to say more, but there's not really much more to the conversation than that. "It was awkward, but there was so much going on, I didn't think any more of it."

"Yes, there were other things to think on, just like there are now," he says, reaching around to grab my ass and pull me close, the previous conversation obviously over, and I raise a brow in question. "I know you're looking forward to seeing your family in a few days, but I hope you'll let me get some of your downtime as well."

"I think I can do that, Cowboy. If you're good."

"Oh, give me one night, and I'll show you how good I can be."

He starts to walk off, and heat creeps into my cheeks. I can't believe I'm here blushing like a damn virgin at my age. I've been with plenty of dirty-talking men over the years, but there is something about this cowboy that has me feeling things I never expected. I still haven't decided what I'm going to do after the Boulder Ranch events, but one thing is for certain, Reggie Junior Thompson will get his one night.

I FEEL LIKE A HORSE'S ASS

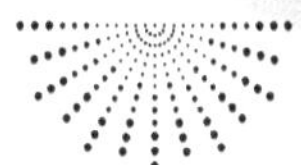

Junior

"Why are you hiding outside?" Jordan asks as she walks up the porch steps of our parents' house. "Have you even made it inside yet?"

"Of course, Sunflower. I think momma can smell me as soon as I make it to town."

"I mean, you do smell like farm animals and manure."

She tries to run past me, and I grab her around the legs, pulling her into a bearhug before she can hit the porch face first. I start tickling her, and she pounds on my arms and back, making sure to not strike anywhere that might do real harm.

"I smell like manure, huh?" I wrap my arm around her head, so her nose is buried in my pit.

"Let me go, jerk," she yells, but I can hear the laughter in her voice. "Okay, okay, I'm sorry. You don't smell like manure." I release her, and she scoots back away from me to the other side of the stairs where she sits trying to catch her breath. "You smell like a horse's ass!" She turns and runs toward the entry, jerking open the storm door before the words have left her lips. I don't even bother trying to chase her down. I kind of feel like a horse's ass. The door clicks closed, and her feet softly pad in my direction. "Bubba, what's wrong?"

I shake my head. I don't want to talk to my baby sister about my love life, or rather sex life, or rather whatever the fuck this is going on between Joanna and me. "I'm fine. The rodeo opens tomorrow, and our team competes, truly competes, for the first time on Saturday."

"Okay," she says, drawing out the word like she doesn't believe me. "That happens every year, and you're always excited, rambling on about how well everyone has been performing in all the exhibitions. Have they sucked this year?"

"No," I say with a small snort. "They're all doing really well."

"Then what the hell has your nuts twisted?"

My brows furrow, and I stare at her like she's grown twelve heads. "What the fuck, Jordan? Where'd you learn that saying from?"

She waves her hand dismissively, and I blow out a long puff of air. Her face softens, and she sits next to me, knocking her shoulder against me before snaking her arm around mine. "Joking aside, what's bothering you?"

I give her a wry smile before turning my attention back to the beer in my hands. Peeling the label off the bottle, I start telling her about the situation with Joanna.

"Taylor's Joanna? The one who went to work for you?"

I nod slowly before taking a long pull from my beer. "I really like her, Sunflower, maybe more than like her, but it's complicated." She looks at me with a brow lifted. "Don't look at me like that. You know that I've had to work my ass off to get this position, and I'm her fucking boss. Not to mention the fact that she left home to find herself and her independence, not to find a relationship for fuck's sake. Hell, I don't even know if this is a relationship. I just know I think about her all day every day, and it's killing me. The worst part is not knowing if she's going to come back to the ranch with me once this weekend's over or stay home."

"Have you told her how you feel? Have you asked her to come back?"

"Well, no. I want it to be her decision. The job was a trial run."

"Do you want her to go back to the ranch with you?"

"Well, yeah, she's been great at her job with the horses and with the team."

"Don't be dumb! That's not what I mean, and you know it."

"I don't know that I want to go back without her. I mean, I will, but I sure as hell won't want to. You know?"

"Then tell her how you feel, Bubba. Don't make her try to read your mind because if your signals are anywhere near as crossed as your answers to my questions, she's probably all confused." She pats my arm and then stands. "I'm going in to get some dinner. I'm starving." Suddenly, she wraps her arms around my shoulders from behind. "I love you, big brother. You deserve to find happiness in more than just your work. If Joanna makes you happy and fills some part of you that's felt empty, then put as much energy into making things work with her as you have into your career."

I don't know what to say to that. When did Jordan get so damn wise? And what the hell does she know about relationships? She's right, though. I need to decide what I want and go for it the same as I've done everything else in my life.

*J*unior

The house is quiet without Jordan. She went home two hours ago, and I've been lying in bed at least half that time just staring at the ceiling. My sister may be a pain in the ass, but having her around at least keeps me out of my own head. Now, I have nothing to distract me from thinking about Fancy.

She was all smiles when I dropped her off at her father's house yesterday. It nearly killed me to watch her climb the stairs and disappear behind the door. I couldn't even bring myself to go inside and say hi to Taylor. I'm sure I'll get an earful about my rudeness from her later, but she'll get over it. I'm not sure if I'll get over Joanna deciding to stay here rather than return to the ranch when we leave in a couple days.

For the third time in the past half hour, I pick up my phone and open my call log. We've not talked on the phone much at all since that day we drove across the mountains back in January, but my finger hovers over her name. With a groan, I slam the phone down on the bed next to me and take in a couple deep breaths.

The woman just returned home after months away, Reg. Let her have some space! I try to negotiate with myself, try to understand that she needs some time with her family. I mean, I just spent the evening with mine. Okay, maybe I spent the evening out on the porch in proximity to mine, but that should count as the same thing, right? *Right?* With a sigh, I pick up the phone and then put it down again. *It's nearly midnight. Whatever you have to say can wait until tomorrow.*

Finally, after an hour of fighting with myself, I put the phone on the bedside table and let myself drift off toward sleep. When my phone dings with an incoming text message, I nearly knock it and the table onto the floor, along with the lamp and the alarm clock my parents insist stay "just in case."

"Jesus Christ," I say, the words coming out much louder than the whisper I'd intended, as I make sure everything is safely where it should be and grab my phone. I listen to the silent house, trying to make sure I didn't wake my parents before looking at the screen. My heart jumps at the sight of her name.

25

TELL ME ABOUT IT

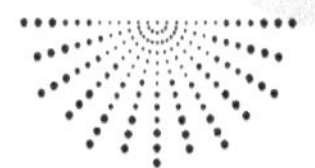

*J*oanna

It feels so good to be home. I'd be lying if I said it didn't feel weird to sleep in my old bedroom last night. The past four months have been like an adventure-filled dream I haven't wanted to wake up from. Now that I'm back, though, I have mixed feelings. This is the end of the road.

Shadows move across the wall as clouds drift across the moon, and my mind flies back to that first winter storm on the Dougherty ranch. I watched the clouds drifting in but didn't think much about them. Thank goodness Junior came looking for me.

The thought of his name conjures other memories. That chaste kiss outside this house. Our trip to the grocery store and that no-so-chaste kiss outside the library. Me on my knees in his cabin and him tied to his chair while I got myself off on his desk. I shake my head, that is not a rabbit hole I need to be going down when it's nearly midnight, and opening ceremony is tomorrow. Still, I can't get him off my mind. The look on his face when he dropped me off yesterday, and the way he took off before I was barely at the door still has my heart in a vise. What was that look?

I pick up my phone from the nightstand and check the time.

157

It's 11:30, and everything but my mind is quiet. I open my messaging app and click on Junior's name.

ME: You up?

As soon as I hit the send button, I inwardly scream at myself. I should have at least apologized for texting so late or told him it wasn't anything urgent.

ME: Sorry. It's nothing urgent, so don't panic if you don't see this until mor

I don't get the chance to even finish the message and hit send before his three dots pop up on my screen. *Shit.* I backspace through the entire thing.

Junior Thompson: Yeah, I'm up. Everything alright?

I laugh at his full name staring me in the face. I've not used his full name in months, and the last time we were alone, he wanted me to call him by the name his family uses. Reggie Junior Thompson is the primary reason my mind won't shut up. He's changed everything. I wanted to get away, to run from everything holding me in place, but he's making it so hard to think of what might come next.

Junior Thompson: Joanna?

The phone pings again, this time with him calling me "Fancy." That fucking nickname was the start of it all. That fucking kiss that I can't seem to forget. I'm the least fancy person I know, and yet the word from his lips makes me want to be fancy, to stand out and hold his attention. Before I can focus enough to type a response, the phone rings in my hand. A smile creeps across my face as I accept the call.

"Hey, are you okay? You sent me a text but didn't respond."

"I thought you'd be sleeping."

"That didn't answer my question, Joanna. Are you alright?"

I nod in the dark, knowing he can't see me. Then I let out a deep breath. "Yes, I'm alright. It's just been a busy day," I hedge.

"Tell me about it," he says quietly.

"Wait, was there a problem at Boulder Ranch today? Is your family okay?"

He laughs. "No, Fancy. I was asking you to tell me about your day."

"Oh!" I don't know what else to say. I wasn't expecting that answer. "Um...I don't want to keep you awake for that."

"I was awake anyway. I'd rather listen to you than count the cracks in the ceiling of this old house."

"Well, I spent half the day at the store with my pa. He's still hating the electronic bookkeeping, but he's using the computer, at least. Then I went over to Gretna House to hang out with Morgan and Taylor. I still can't believe Morgan named the bed and breakfast after her bitchy ass grandmother. Oh, and Taylor's pissed at you for not coming in to say hello yesterday, by the way."

He groans. "I figured that. Between her and Jordan, I never get a moment's peace. Fucking little sisters!"

A laugh escapes me, and I slap my hand over my mouth. I had forgotten where I was for a minute, and I don't want to wake Taylor and my pa.

"So, why are you up?" he asks, his voice much softer. I bite my lip, unsure how to answer without putting my entire heart on the line.

*J*unior

I pull the phone away from my ear for a second to look at the screen before holding it back to listen carefully. Finally, I hear her breathing. She'd grown so quiet, I almost thought she'd hung up on me.

"Nerves, I think," she eventually says. "I don't know why. We've done some traveling, and the team has been great, but this weekend feels different."

"Boulder Ranch is different," I concede. "Though I'm from across the county line, Boulder Ranch is home. Every time we come back here, no matter how much faith I have in our team and our riders, I feel like I, personally, have something to prove."

I sigh. "Yeah, maybe that's it."

"What's going on in that beautiful head of yours, Fancy?"

I have a feeling I know, but I don't want to put words in her mouth. I was honest with Jordan earlier. I want Joanna to make this decision on her own no matter how much it's killing me to sit back and wait. I just don't know what I'm going to do if she decides to stay here.

She sighs. "You know, when I first thought about leaving here, I just wanted to escape. That was my primary focus. Now that I've been gone all these months and returned, I don't have the same urge. I don't feel that same weight on my chest."

As she talks, my own chest tightens, and my lungs constrict. She's not going back to Double D with us, with me. Fuck, I can't breathe. "That's a good thing, right?" I somehow manage to say.

"That's the thing. I don't know." Something in her tone eases the pressure that has me holding my chest. There's a sadness there, and I want to hold her through it. Before I can say anything though, she continues on with, "I'm just not sure I belong here anymore, you know?"

"What do you mean? This is your home."

"It will always be home, and I've missed the hell out of my family, but something has changed. Maybe it's me. Maybe I've changed."

I smile in the dark room. "I know what you mean. I felt so guilty when I left home the first time. Of course, my mother and sister were big contributors to that guilt, but still, it was there." I expect her to say something, but she stays quiet. "Every time I came home that first year, I struggled with the changes that were happening in me because everyone else seemed frozen in time. I missed them, but it wasn't enough to make me want to stay. Finally, I just stopped wanting to come back."

She tries to silence her gasp with a cough, but I catch it. I know how that statement sounds. It's not that I don't love my family. I absolutely do, but I also love my freedom and the life that I've built elsewhere. "Please don't think me uncaring. It's not that. I feel the connection to my family and the place that made me who I am. It's there every time I come home. It just doesn't hold my heart like Double D does." I bite my tongue to keep from saying something stupid like 'except maybe now.'

"You know, you never did tell me why you changed your name. Did it have something to do with that disconnect or…"

I don't let her finish. "It was silly, honestly. When I was at my first out-of-town ranch, the guys would make fun of me, saying my name wasn't country enough. They'd say I didn't belong on a ranch."

"That's ridiculous. What the hell does your name have to do with anything?"

"Well, it wasn't just my name, but the name was the easiest thing to deal with. So, when the Doughertys hired me, I told everyone to call me Junior."

"Okay. I get that."

"Well, it also made it easier to not hear my father's name all the time. The Dougherty brothers love to call everyone by their full names, so I was always Reggie Thompson before I asked them to call me Junior too. Now, even after all these years, I'm still Junior Thompson without deviation."

"I can see you in both names," she says, and my cock twitches at the thought of her shouting my name, my real name, when she comes.

"Yeah. It's like me calling you Fancy."

"That's not the same," she counters with a chuckle.

"Isn't it, though? You're Fancy when we're alone." Her exhale comes through the phone, and I hope it's a sign that she's still considering the possibility of us. I have to believe she's going to come back to Double D with us.

"Thanks for talking to me. Sorry for keeping you up."

"You never have to apologize to me. If you need me, I'm here."

Neither of us say anything else for several moments. I want to tell her that my promise stands even if she decides to stay, but I can't bring myself to say the words. I won't be the one who makes it real.

"Thanks. I'll see you tomorrow."

"Oh, and Joanna."

"Yeah," she says with an eagerness that has my stomach clenching.

"Everyone goes out after the opening ceremony, so be ready for a night out."

"Is that an order, bossman?"

I let out a quiet laugh, held in only so I don't wake the house. "Yes, Fancy, it is."

26

HOW CAN I AVOID YOU?

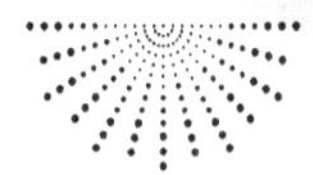

*J*oanna

The opening ceremony is relatively low key, and the exhibition events have been fun to watch. Because our team isn't participating tonight, and I didn't have to worry about getting covered in horse shit, I opted to dress up a little. Knee-high boots, a skirt that comes to mid-thigh, and a leather peacoat. I even left my hair down rather than pulling it up in my signature ponytail. I won't say I'm trying to catch someone's eye, but the heat of Junior's stare as soon as I join the team on the arena floor says I made the right choice.

I'm standing near the back of the bleachers when I feel him come up behind me. The air shifts, and my skin tingles. When his hand touches my waist, my heart rate jumps.

"Hey there, Fancy. I was wondering where you'd disappeared to after the opening."

I don't respond, just stand there with him pressed up against me, his thumb making small circles on my back. His breath tickles my ear, and I close my eyes against the sensation. The desire to turn around in his arms and press my lips to his is near impossible to ignore until Kelly's voice carries over the crowd. Junior takes a step back, hesitating a moment before removing his hand from my waist.

"What's up bossman, Joanna? Y'all gonna join us as at The Thirsty Pony?"

"You know that's not my scene, Kells," Junior says as I turn around to face our barn manager who only came out for the opening events and will be returning to the ranch after tomorrow's events.

"I'll probably head back home to our farm before tomorrow's go time," I respond with a shrug. "It's been nice having a couple days off to spend with my family and friends."

Kelly looks between the two of us where we still stand close to one another, and her eyes narrow. I make sure to keep my eyes on hers. Somehow, I know that if I demure, she'll take that as a sign to fish for more information. She can guess there's something going on between us, but I'm not going to give away anything before he and I figure out what we're going to do about it. Finally, after what seems like forever, she relaxes her gaze. "Bunch of old ass ninnies. If you change your minds, you know where we'll be," she says and walks away.

"And we'll be anywhere else but there," Junior says under his breath.

I smile up at him. "Oh really? And where are we going, Mr. Thompson?"

He rolls his eyes. "Don't call me that. Makes me sound like my dad. Shit, call me Reggie in front of the whole world before you call me Mr. Thompson."

"Would Mr. Thompson join his team at The Thirsty Pony?"

He shakes his head and lets out a small chuckle. "Let's go, and I'll tell you on the way."

"I have my car, remember?"

"Shit, no. I forgot."

"Don't worry. I'll ask Jacob to come get it if you don't think we'll make it back until real late."

He opens the door to his truck and leans in close as I turn to climb in. I stare into his dark eyes, the colors of the setting sun reflecting in them. "If things go well, we won't be back until tomorrow afternoon." I pull out my phone and text my brother to come by and take the car back to the house. I have to assure him I'm fine and that I won't leave town without saying goodbye.

"Everything good?" Junior asks when he gets into the truck.

"Yeah, I just had to promise Jacob my first born." I try to hold in a laugh but completely lose it when his mouth drops open. "Your face was priceless," I manage to wheeze out between breaths.

"Oh Fancy, you must want to be on your worst behavior tonight, huh?"

I sober at his question, though a jolt of heat goes straight to my core. "Where are we going?" I ask before my strained breathing can betray me.

"We're going dancing like everyone else, just not where they're going."

I tilt my head and narrow my eyes when he turns away from town and toward the mountains.

As I watch him climb onto the mechanical bull in this dive bar, I wonder how I never knew this place existed. Reggie, as he asked me to call him for tonight, said Spurs has been in Harper's Hallow for years. Just goes to show how much I've kept myself sheltered all these years. When the bull starts moving forward and backward, all my thoughts return to him. His body moves seamlessly with the apparatus, as if the jerky movements and simulated bucking were his natural environment. Now, I see why he had wanted to be a bronc rider. Fuck, he's fluid like he was built for the ride. And that thought has me squeezing my thighs together.

After the sexiest eight seconds I've ever watched, he climbs down from the bull and heads my way with a huge smile. "Your turn, Fancy."

I shake my head vigorously, though I can't hide the smile on my face at his joy. "There's no way I can follow that."

He leans in close after jumping over the side of the pen like we're not in our mid-thirties. "What's that?"

"That...that porn you just made," I blurt, suddenly glad the bar is dimly lit because I know my cheeks are crimson. *Why in the hell does this man make me blush like a schoolgirl?*

"Oh, Fancy, if I were to make a porn tonight, I'd be riding something softer than a mechanical bull. Now, let me see what you can do." He slaps my ass and leads me to the entrance for the bull's pen. All I can think is that I'm so worked up from watching him that if I last eight seconds on this fucking bull, I'm going to come all over it.

"I can't do this right now, Reggie."

"Are you gonna ride or not," the guy running the bull asks. "There are others waiting."

I look back at Reggie, hoping he catches the plea in my eyes. "Let someone else go. We'll be back in a bit." The guy shrugs his shoulders and waves over some young chick who pulls the hat off the guy she's with.

"Let's dance instead," I say, grabbing his hand and pulling him toward the dance floor. Dancing is a much safer activity. At least, I hope line dancing will distract my brain from the need between my legs.

At first, he tries to pull me close, but I drag him out to the middle of the line where we have to follow the others or get trampled. It's a struggle to keep up with some of the new steps I don't know, but I'm grateful for the distraction. When the music slows, though, he wraps his arms around me from behind and pulls me to the outside corner of the dance floor.

"Are you trying to avoid me, Fancy?"

I turn to face him, putting my hands up around his neck as he puts his one leg between mine, pulling me close. Of course, just when I was getting control over my libido, he's here between my legs, grinding my control into submission.

"How can I avoid you, Cowboy," I coo in a way I hope sounds more disgruntled than frustrated. He chuckles, so I continue, probably making this worse. "You've taken up permanent residence in my thoughts, and your presence is impossible to ignore." He leans down and runs his nose up my neck until he gets to my earlobe and nips at it. I whimper, feeling my desire coat my inner thighs. When the music changes, I let out a sigh, thinking he's going to release me, but he doesn't.

"You're soaking through my jeans, Fancy. Why are you too stubborn to just tell me it's time to take you to bed?"

I look up into his eyes and open my mouth to speak. I don't know what I'll say, but I have to say something. A spotlight swings around onto the dance floor, pulling his gaze away. His eyes bulge, and then they narrow with laughter as he says, "Would you look at that."

I turn around in his arms, wondering what in the hell managed to pull his attention from me, and I'm caught. At some point during our moment, the DJ switched up the music, putting on She Thinks My Tractor's Sexy, and rather than the dance floor being full, one man stands in the middle of the floor gyrating. Mirth bubbles up from my toes as I watch Old Man Wilber move around the dance floor like a drunk chicken on baby deer legs. I think back to Morgan's story of her and Jacob on the back of Wilber's haunted trail ride during the Fall Festival, and I double over with laughter. Eventually, he grabs some poor girl's hand to dance with him, and the floor fills with people.

Reggie tugs on my wrist, and we leave, both of us still laughing when we get to his truck. "It's time I get you alone," he says, hedging me in against his truck. My mouth opens, and he wastes no time capturing it with his own, his tongue lapping mine until he pulls a moan from my lips. "Get in," he rasps, stepping back from me. I take in a deep breath before reaching up and pulling myself into the cab, letting him close the door.

TRY ME, COWBOY

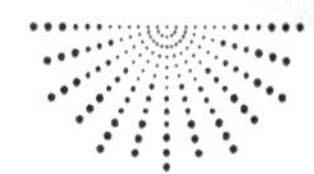

*J*unior

I have never before been so happy to have planned ahead. When I reserved the room two days ago and picked up the keycard yesterday, I was still worried something would go wrong, and she wouldn't be with me. Now that she's here, and we're on the elevator without having to stop at the registration desk, it was worth the drive up and back. I hold her close against me, though every graze of her body against mine has my cock uncomfortably hard behind my zipper.

This entire night. Every move. Every breath. Every touch. Every damn time our eyes have locked has been nothing more than one long edging session, and I don't know who's more wound up. What I do know is that I have to somehow convince her to return to the ranch. I'm not ready to let her go. I don't think I'll ever be ready to let her go.

As soon as I let us in the room, she grabs my shirt and leans into me. My heart jolts with the contact. I look down into her stormy blue eyes and my breath catches. This woman is strong and yet sensitive, passionate and empathetic, beautiful and humble. She's absolutely perfect, and I can't get enough.

I turn us around, so her back is against the wall and raise a hand to cup her cheek. "Joanna…"

"Shhh," she says, holding a finger up to my lips. "I didn't get to ride that bull tonight, but I have every intention of riding you, Cowboy." Her hand reaches behind my neck, pulling my mouth to hers. I let her and lose myself in the kiss.

My hands slide the jacket off her shoulders before I peel off her shirt. I pull back from the kiss, taking a moment to enjoy the rise and fall of her chest, breasts lifted in the black lace bra she's wearing. There's nothing practical about this bra, and I can't wait to see the panties she's put on with it. A thrill runs up my spine at the realization that she's just as excited for tonight as I am.

"Did you wear this for me?" I ask, kissing over her jaw and nipping at her nipple through the lace. She shudders, her fingers grasping at my tight curls. "I'm going to take that as a yes," I drawl, reaching around her waist to unbutton the skirt that's keeping me from seeing what else she's hiding. When my hands slide down around her ass to find she's in nothing more than a thong, my cock swells uncomfortably hard, and I groan. "Fuck, Fancy, you're going to be my undoing."

"Don't worry, Cowboy, I'll put you back together when I'm done."

With a growl, I grip under her ass cheeks and lift her until she wraps her thick thighs around my waist. Walking us toward the bed, I lick along her clavicle and suck on her neck.

"No branding me," she says, her voice breathy. "At least not somewhere visible."

I smile against her shoulder and then toss her on the bed. After a quick squeak of surprise, she laughs before scooting herself back to watch me. I pull off my shirt, not bothering to unbutton it, and she licks her lips. When I slip off my boots and push down my jeans and boxers at the same time, she bites her lip.

"Damn, Cowboy, you look delicious."

She's a vision splayed out on the bed in black lingerie and knee-high boots. My cock stands straight out pointing the way to her like a damn divining rod. Before I can move onto the bed, though, she's gotten onto her hands and knees, crawling toward me, her eyes holding mine. When she takes me in her mouth, my eyes roll back. I fist both hands in her hair and moan her name. My hips work back and forth, pushing my cock down her throat, and she takes it like a fucking goddess.

"Fuck, that mouth of yours is so fucking hot!" She reaches up and grips my ass, and her fingers press in hard, urging me faster. "Oh, you want me to fuck your mouth hard, do you?" Her eyes look up again, pleading, and I give in to her until saliva is coating my dick and running down the sides of her mouth. "You're so fucking perfect, Fancy, so fucking goddamned perfect." I pull my cock from her mouth and lift her torso until she's pressed against me, her mouth close enough for me to capture it with my own. Using my thumbs, I wipe the drool from her chin and kiss her softly.

I gently push her backwards until she's once again laid out before me. Climbing onto the bed, I slowly kiss my way up her legs. As I suck on her inner thighs, spreading them out to make room for myself, she squirms. And when I press my chin up and down the lace front of the panties that barely cover her already drenched pussy, she starts writhing.

I chuckle against her soft mound when she stammers out bits of the names she calls me, never getting one of them fully correct. "Mmm Jun…" I pull her panties to the side and flick my tongue against her already swollen clit. "Fuck, Cow…" Then I wrap my lips around the tight bud and suck. "Shit, Regggg…" Slipping two fingers inside her, all words become incoherent as she bucks against my face, riding my hand like a steed.

"That's it, Joanna, come for me. Ride my fingers and face like you're gonna ride my cock."

Her head is thrown back, and with one hand, she squeezes her breast while the other grips the blanket. I work my fingers in and out of her, making sure to curl them just enough to hit the ridge on the inside while my tongue continues its assault on her clit. Within seconds, she's squeezing my fingers and screaming her release. I soak in every sound and lap up every drop before I kiss my way up the rest of her body. Without warning, I flip us over, so she's straddling my hips.

She's still in a daze from her orgasm, her eyes glazed over and breaths heavy. "Are you ready for this ride, Fancy? I promise it'll last more than eight seconds." She smiles seductively and then reaches between us to line my cock up with her entrance before fully seating herself in the saddle. Grabbing my Stetson from where it had fallen off when she gripped my head between her thighs, she sets it on her own head and winks.

"Try me, Cowboy," she finally says.

It's sexy as fuck, and I waste no time giving her the ride of her life.

*J*oanna

There is something about laying in Reggie's arms that soothes my soul. My mind might be running a mile a minute, but my soul is calm. The anxiety that has been racking my body these past couple days is gone. The confusion and uncertainty about the future is still there, but it's not debilitating. His body pressed up against mine just feels right.

He whispers my name in his sleep, and my heart flutters. It's too late to question my feelings for this man or to try and stop them. They've been barreling forward since that mistletoe kiss, maybe since that day I found him standing in my store. He's so much more than just the physical appearance that took my breath away that day. He's even more than the ambitious rodeo team leader who keeps us all in check. He's kind and gentle. He listens to understand. He gives as well as he takes. He's everything a girl could wish for, but I'm no longer a girl.

If I were, there'd be no question of whether or not I'd run away with him back to Double D Ranch. I'd throw caution to the wind and take my chances, but I'm a grown woman. I need more than just a beautiful smile and hard dick to fall onto. I need to belong. I need to be needed and wanted. I want to feel like what I'm doing not only matters but also makes me happy.

Working with the horses does make me happy. It's hard labor, but I've not felt so satisfied with a day's work as I do when I fall into bed exhausted after a day in the barn. I work with a great team, and they've made me feel at home. But Double D is not my home. Home means family, and they're all here.

Reggie shifts in his sleep and pulls me tighter against him. I smile. He's the unknown in this whole equation. Obviously, he wants me. There's never been a lack of attraction between us. I can't help but wonder, though, if there's anything more to it. This is the weekend I decide to stay in Cole County or return to Double D, and he's not mentioned it once. Does that mean he doesn't care if I stay?

I turn in his arms, trying my damnedest not to wake him. He stirs slightly, but I throw my leg over his, and a quiet smile settles over his lips. His eyes never open, and his breaths even back out. I take in the contours of his face. My fingers itch to rub along his trimmed beard. His hand slides down from where it had sat at my waist and loosely cups my ass. His face blurs as a single tear runs down the side of my face. I lean forward and press my lips to his cheek as my heart makes the decision for me. I want to be wherever he is. I just need him to want me there too.

DON'T PLAY DUMB!

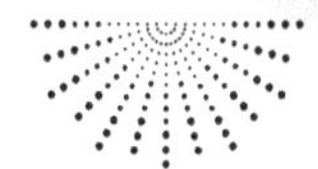

*J*oanna

Sun streams through the curtain, illuminating the hotel room. Reggie's arm is draped over my midsection, and his legs are entwined with mine. Warmth floods my entire body at the connection, at the fact that he hasn't disentangled himself or turned away. We still haven't talked about what happens next, and I'm afraid to broach the subject. Here, in this room, far away from work and our team, it's easy to just put it all away and pretend like there isn't a looming cloud.

His hand slides up, tracing the roundness of my stomach and up to my chest. I love the feel of his rough palms on my skin and how his large hands fully cover my breast. My nipple hardens at his touch. He kisses my shoulder, and heat courses from the spot straight to my core.

"What's going on in that beautiful head of yours, Fancy?"

A smile blooms on my face. He is the best distraction. "Just thinking how much work there is to do today."

"We have time," he says, shifting himself until he's poised between my legs. I bite my lip as his hardness presses against my center. His tongue flicks my nipple, and a ripple of desire pulses through me. I lift my hips to increase the contact, and he chuckles. "I thought you were in a rush to go." He slides his cock between my lips, the friction against my clit eliciting a moan I can't contain.

"Reg..."

I don't get the words out before his lips capture mine. My hands travel down his sides to cup his ass, the muscles squeezing beneath my fingers as he continues to slide against me. Reaching between us, I grip his cock, and he groans. I waste no time in lifting my hips further, wrapping my legs higher around his hips for leverage, and notching him at my entrance.

"So impatient," he teases when he finally pulls back from the kiss.

I glower at him, and he chuckles again, his muscles rippling, and the tip of his cock begins that delicious stretch it does every time he enters me, but then it stops. How he holds himself back from plunging in, I don't know. It's infuriating when my core is aching for him. Once again, I reach for his hips, and he *tsks* at me. A growl of frustration comes from my lips.

"Tell me what you want, Fancy."

I try to glare at him, but he moves a little further inside, and I whimper instead. "Fuck," is all I manage to say for several second as he slides in at an achingly slow pace. He raises a brow. "Me. Fuck me!"

Finally, he does, and I hold onto him like a lifeline, trying my damnedest to keep my emotions at bay as he wrings multiple orgasms from my body.

We arrive at Boulder Ranch not long after noon. Between checking out of the hotel and grabbing food, we got a later start than I had wanted. Not that I'm complaining about the reason for our delay, but I really wanted to be here earlier to exercise the horses and get them ready for this evening.

As we enter the barn, I go through my mental checklist of things I need to get done for each of the horses, especially Clementine. I need to make sure her legs are wrapped before Chloe gets here for warmups. I stop short at Clementine's stall when she doesn't approach the door or greet me.

"What's wrong, girl?" I say softly. Her eyes are pained, and she stands stock still.

"What the matter?" Reggie asks from where he stopped about twenty feet away and is watching out the side door.

"Something's wrong with Clementine," I say and pull open the stall door. "What the…" Reggie walks up behind me and grabs my arm before I rush into the stall. "Someone already wrapped her legs. Who else has been here?" Clementine snorts and paws at the ground with one of her hooves before groaning. I try to take a step forward, but Reggie holds me in place.

"Wait," he says. "If she's in pain, she could hurt you. That's what happened during the holidays."

"With fucking Jerry?" I retort. Reggie's eyes turn back toward where he had been watching out the door earlier. "What?" I ask, and Clementine groans again.

"I caught sight of Jerry outside the barn as we were coming in and thought it strange he didn't come greet us."

I pull my arm from his hand and step forward. "If that fucker hurt her, I'm going to hurt him."

"Be careful," he says from my side, but he doesn't try to stop me.

Clementine shakes her head, and I hold up my hands. My tone is soft as I try to keep her calm on my approach. "It's me, girl," I say as I reach out to caress her head and pat down her neck. "Can I check your legs?" She doesn't move, just stares at me, and the pain in her eyes guts me. "Let me make it better," I coax, sliding my hands down her legs and stopping right above the tape. Reggie grabs Clementine's halter to hold her steady for me. I give him a soft smile and find the end of the wrap. When I start to unwind it, she snorts, and Reggie talks to her, trying to distract her from any pain my work might cause.

At first, I don't see anything wrong with her wraps. They're done properly and there doesn't seem to be any visible injuries under the tape. As I begin the final few rounds near her ankle, I gasp. "There's something hard in her wrap," I say, keeping my touch light. I hold my hand at the base of the wrap as I finish unwinding it, and wince as two sharp burrs fall into my palm.

"What the fuck?" Reggie exclaims and then has to soothe Clementine all over again. "Sorry, girl."

I move to her other leg and undo that wrap. There are two more burrs on that side. My blood boils. "I'm going to kill him! I may make him eat these fucking things," I say, holding the pods in my hand. I'm too angry to be bothered by the pricks in my palm.

"Hold on there, Fancy. We don't know for sure who it was. Let me see if the Garrison's have a good camera angle."

Twenty minutes later, I've brushed down Clementine, making sure she's no longer in pain, and taken her for a walk around the outer pen. We've just returned to her stall when Jerry walks into the barn. I take one look at him and see red. I don't even wait for Reggie to return, nor do I look to see if anyone else is around. My feet take me directly toward him.

"You son of a bitch!" I hiss. "How dare you!"

Jerry turns at my words. At first, his expression is simple shock, and then his stare hardens. "What are you talking about?"

"Don't play dumb, Jerry." I take a step closer. "Why did Clementine kick you all those months ago? Why did you try so hard to get her away from me that night of the storm? Why the fuck were you here so early messing with my horse?"

He scoffs. "Your horse? You do know you don't own her, right?" He takes a step toward me but pulls up short, his eyes catching on something over my shoulder.

"She doesn't, but I do." Reggie's tone holds a hint of malice I've never heard from him.

Jerry shakes his head. "I don't know why she's here attacking me."

"Cut the shit," Reggie says. "I just watched the camera footage, and you're the only one who's been in Clementine's stall since we left last night."

"I'm part of the team. I'm here doing my job."

"Clementine isn't part of your job. She hasn't been for months now."

"I was just..." He's cut off by a female voice coming from the entrance.

"Babe? Did you take care of that hor..." Tricia, a barrel racer from another team, stops short, falling silent, when she sees the three of us standing here.

I don't think. I swing. When Reggie grabs me around my waist, pulling me against his chest, Jerry's on the ground, hay clinging to his clothes, and blood running down his face. Tricia gasps and turns to run, but the Garrison brothers are standing at the door, blocking her exit. Neither Jerry nor Tricia will ever hurt a horse again.

DON'T PRETEND

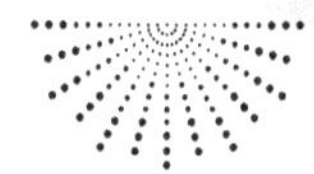

*J*oanna

I hold my breath as Clementine and her rider bolt around the barrels. The clock is ticking far too fast, and though she's running a flawless race, it's going to be close. I've spent most of my life around horses, but I've never felt as close to one as Clementine, and I love watching her compete almost as much as I love riding her myself. To know that someone had tried to hurt her just hours before this race has me tied in knots.

"You can breathe, Joanna. She's running fine," Kelly says from my side. She'll be heading back to the ranch with the rest of the caravan once today's events are over.

"I know, Kells. She's come such a long way."

"You had a lot to do with that, you know, even before you realized something was wrong this afternoon."

I turn my face toward her, knowing there's something more to this conversation than her simply giving a pep talk. She's not a pep talk kind of woman. Kelly Anderson is more of a kick-you-in-the-gut kind of woman who will take you for burgers and a beer after you've thrown up breakfast on her shoes. I raise a brow.

"Your trial period's over, Joanna. There's something going on between you and the bossman that's likely complicating any decision you need to make. Junior Thompson is a good man. We've had women come and go from the ranch, and he's never bat an eye, never been distracted from the path he set out for himself years ago."

I purse my lips, unsure where this is going. "What are you trying to say, Kells?"

"I'm not trying to say anything. I'm telling you straight forward. You've been a damn good addition to our team. You've had a positive influence on the people and animals. You're also good for Junior. Those things don't have to be in competition." When I just stare at her, she gives me a half smile and shakes her head. "You got a lot of try in you. I hope you put that energy into excitement for the future instead of fear of the past." Without another word, she walks off toward the holding pens.

She's not wrong. This thing between Junior Thompson and me is complicating my decision. I've come to love the team, and I surely love the animals, especially Clementine. But I'm also falling for Junior. I can't just decide to stay without knowing where he and I stand. I don't want to be stuck with a broken heart, else I might as well stay home. Junior's heat penetrates my back before I hear him whispering in my ear.

"Your girl just won. Why do you look so serious?"

I turn myself, so I can look at him clearly. The man is beautiful, and I ache to wrap my arms around his waist. But today, in this place, he's my boss. I look down, afraid he'll catch the sadness welling in my eyes. He puts his finger under my chin and forces me to look back at him.

"What's wrong, Fancy?"

I give him a tight smile, still trying to play off the emotions threatening to spew all over him. "I'm not good at this."

"At what? Talk to me. Do we need to go sit in the truck?"

His demeanor screams how badly he wants to pull me into his arms, the way his hands rub up and down from my elbows to my shoulders. But he doesn't. He can't. I shake my head.

"I should go make sure Clementine's taken care of and ready to roll."

I start to pull away, but he grabs my wrists.

"Joanna, talk to me."

Taking a deep breath, I think about all the things I want to say. None of them seem right for this moment. Maybe we should have talked things through this morning before we left the hotel. Maybe the time we spent on that last round of sex on the decorative chair in the corner of the room would've been better used to discuss how we move forward.

"What do you want from me?" I choke out.

He shakes his head as if slapped. "What do you mean? I realize something is wrong, and I want you to talk to me? Did something happen since I took you to get your car?" He whispers that last question, and that small shift in tone is enough to make the tears fall.

I'm not one to cry. I've not cried much since I was a little girl, not even after my ma passed. Crying makes me feel weak and vulnerable, and, honestly, it pisses me the fuck off. Unfortunately for Junior, he gets that anger.

"No, I mean, what do you actually want from me, with me, what the fuck ever you want to call it." I drop my voice when I realize heads are turning our way. "We're both standing here wanting to put our arms around each other, but we can't. You whispered the part about dropping me at my car like it was some big secret because it is. But part of my reason for leaving Cole County in the first place was to stop pretending I was okay when I wasn't. I'm not okay with pretending I don't have feelings for you, which will make it very hard to pretend you are nothing more than my boss if I go back to the ranch."

Worry creases his brow. I've seen that look many times over the last month as we watched our newest riders compete and even before when we planned that first exhibition at the ranch. Finally, after an excruciating span of seconds, his eyes soften, and he responds. "Then don't."

My head spins, and it feels like my chest cracks open. I throw a hand over my mouth to stifle the sob, and I stare at him with wide eyes. He said it so easily, like he hadn't wanted me back at the ranch anyway and was doing me a favor. Blinking my eyes rapidly to clear the unwanted tears and the haze of surprise, I take a step away from him.

"Fancy," he says, putting his hands on either side of my face.

"No, don't. I think my time here is done. I'll head home." My voice is much calmer than I feel.

"Joanna, stop," he says much more forcefully, as I turn away. "I meant don't pretend." I stop in my tracks. Turning back to face him, I see the majority of our team standing around near the spectacle we're making. "Don't pretend you don't have feelings for me because I can't hide mine. Don't pretend I'm nothing more than your boss because, woman, you've run every damn thing since you arrived." He takes a step toward me. "And please don't pretend that when you come back to the ranch, you're moving back into the barracks because I don't want to ever wake up again without you next to me."

The knot in my throat is so thick, I can hardly breathe let alone speak. Tears flow freely down my cheeks, and I'm stuck to the ground like someone put glue on my boots.

"I don't want you to pretend any of it, Fancy. Just say you're coming back, and we'll work the rest out. Won't we, team?"

A cheer goes up around us, almost louder than the cheers of those in the stands still watching the arena. I look around at the faces of my new friends, and I catch my family standing behind them. Morgan and Taylor both have wet faces. Then, my eyes land on Kelly, and the stoic hard ass wipes under her eye. When I make a full turn back around to the man who not only made my dream come true but also worked his way into my dreams, I smile. He opens his arms, and I walk into them.

After a few moments of just soaking in his scent and presence while he whispers affirmations of love and promises for the future in my ear, I turn around to look at everyone.

"Why are y'all just standing around here? Don't you think it's time we get ready to head out?"

Another round of cheers erupts before the group breaks away to pack up the animals and gear. I grab Junior's hand and pull him toward my family. He smiles at Taylor and gives a nod to my pa, but there's a sadness in his eyes. His family never comes. I quickly hug everyone, and he shakes hands with Jacob. We're about to follow the team out to the trailers when we're stopped by a loud cry coming through the exiting crowd.

"Bubba, wait!"

"Reggie, hold on, son."

Confusion glides across Junior's face before it's replaced with relief and finally joy. He turns around and catches Jordan as she barrels into his chest, her arms outstretched like she's a little girl and not a woman in her mid-twenties. His father shakes his hand, and his mom hugs him around Jordan who hasn't yet let go.

"Your team did great, son!"

"Thanks, Pop."

"Hi, Joanna," his mom says, her eyes taking in where Junior has taken my hand again after Jordan finally releases him. She gives me a knowing smile, and I smile back before letting her wrap me in a hug.

"We won't hold you," Mr. Thompson says. "We just wanted to let you know we were here, and we're proud of you."

Junior's eyes are glassy, so I promise that we'll be safe on the drive to the next showcase and each one between here and our return to the ranch. I also promise that we'll call when we arrive. We watch his family walk toward the gate to meet up with mine before they all lift an arm and wave. He gives a little sniffle before waving back.

"You sure you're ready for this ride, Fancy?"

"And every ride until forever."

EPILOGUE

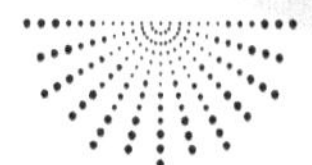

Junior

"They're here," Joanna yells from the other room.

A smile plays along my lips as I dry my hands from where I had been finishing up the breakfast dishes. Normally, on the mornings where I cook, Joanna cleans up, but she'd been so full of nervous energy that I sent her into the other room to finish whatever invisible tasks were running riot through her mind. The house looks amazing. It can't get any cleaner, and the fresh flower arrangements she's set up everywhere have it looking bright and inviting. Regardless, no one is going to worry about all that when they see what else we have planned for their visit. My smile grows as I reach the door and see the two SUVs pulling up the driveway.

I step out onto the porch behind Joanna and put my arms around her waist, letting my chin sit on her shoulder. Jordan and Taylor are out of their respective vehicles before they even fully stop, and both come running our way.

"JD!"

"Bubba!"

They're up the stairs and nearly bowling us down before we can even get out a word of greeting. To see them like this reminds me of when they were young teenagers instead of the 29-year-old women they are. Well, that thought only lasts until each of their boyfriends climb out of the SUVs behind them. I give a nod of acknowledgment to Garrett, but I can barely bring myself to look at Taylor's man. My lip curls. I know my sister has to grow up, but dammit, I don't have to like it, do I?

Joanna slaps my chest, and I pull my attention back to the woman who makes my entire world turn. She's still engulfed in Taylor's arms, but she gives me a look of warning that says *Fix your face, Cowboy*. Taking a deep breath, I relax my scowl and extend my hand to Garrett. Then I do the same with Jordan's boyfriend. I can't even remember what in the hell his name is.

"Nice to see you again," he says. "Thanks for the invitation."

I turn to look at Joanna who shrugs before jumping into her father's arms. Her happiness is palpable, and my heart swells. There's nothing more beautiful than Joanna's joy. Noise from the driveway pulls my attention away from the porch reunion. Within seconds, I'm down the few stairs and crossing to the larger of the two SUVs.

"Hey, Mom. How much stuff did you pack?" I say with a chuckle, wrapping my arms around her from behind.

"Very funny, Reginald," she retorts.

I pull back and place my hand over my heart when she turns around. "Ouch!"

"Come make yourself useful, son," Pops calls from the back of the SUV where he has the back door open and is popping out suitcases and containers that have to be food mom insisted on bringing. When I grab the food containers and sigh, Pops just shrugs. "You know your mom. She wasn't coming emptyhanded."

"Marybeth, can you grab the baby's diaper bag?" A female voice says from the other side of the car.

"Gimme that chubster," Joanna calls back, and I can't hold back my smile. When she starts cooing at the baby, something twists my insides. I never before thought about being a father, but suddenly, the idea of Joanna loving on a child we've made has me nearly doubled over with need.

By the time I help get all the bags in the house, the quiet peacefulness we'd eaten to this morning is a cacophony of voices and disjointed conversations. Taylor's youngest siblings are running through the house, talking a mile a minute about the movie room and the view. My parents are seated at the island chatting with Jordan and Taylor while Morgan sits off to the side with Joanna. I stop in my tracks at the sight of her holding Baby Darren, and the breath whooshes from my lungs. When she catches me staring, she smiles and gestures for me to come over.

"She looks good like that, doesn't she?" Morgan asks, but I can't formulate words. She's stunning.

"Do you wanna hold him?" Joanna asks, as if I'm not wondering how to steal her away from everyone and keep myself buried in her until she's holding one of our own.

I lean down and whisper in her ear. "No, but I want to take you upstairs and make one of our own." I watch as heat climbs her neck and settles in her cheeks. Off to my side, Morgan giggles, earning her a glare from Joanna.

"Since when did you start blushing, Sis?" Jake says, walking up to kiss Morgan on the cheek before sitting next to her. She leans into him with a smile.

"Your house is beautiful," Taylor says, coming to join us. She places a hand on the baby's head, and he stirs in Joanna's arms. "Gimme my grandson," she says with a wink, and I groan. She walks off with the baby toward where my parents and Jordan are sitting on the couches. Jordan's boyfriend sits at her side, and her hand plays in the hair at the back of his head. My blood pressure starts to rise.

Joanna gets up from the island and walks toward the pantry. "Come help with this, Cowboy," she says before disappearing through the entry. I excuse myself and follow her. No sooner to I cross the threshold than she grabs my shirt and pulls me in, her mouth finding mine immediately. My hand slides up to cup her neck, and I deepen the kiss. When she pulls back, I groan, my dick ready for what normally comes next when she initiates. "Calm down, Cowboy. You looked like you were ready to attack multiple people out there."

I sigh and lean my forehead against hers. She reads me so well. "I know I'm not home often. I know I've been out here living my life and pretending like everything at home has just remained as I left it. I know," I growl out in frustration, "that my two little sisters have grown up, but damn if it's easy to accept."

She leans up and kisses my nose. "Ask Jake, or better yet, ask Morgan, how he reacted to me even talking to a guy at the Fall Festival one year. I think there must be some ingrained aggression toward any man who approaches a sister that all brothers feel." She steps back until she's up against the countertop and pulls me with her. "They're smart women. They've found good men. Be happy for them." She gives me a bright smile and links her hands behind my neck. "Besides, you have to make your own happy announcement soon."

"I do," I say, pressing my lips to hers. "We should probably go do that."

*J*oanna

Kelly should arrive any minute now, and my skin is prickly with anticipation. Once everyone had settled in, I made the announcement that I'd like to get a few group photos made out on the balcony. So, everyone took off toward their rooms to get ready. Reggie's parents eyed us curiously as they climbed the stairs, but I just kept a neutral smile on my face until they were out of sight. Somehow, we'd managed to keep everyone inside the house, so they couldn't see the surprise out on the grounds behind the house.

Reggie heads out back when we get the text that Kelly has arrived with the photographers. One will be on the ground and the other on the main level to get everyone prepared on the balcony. My hands sweat as I stand just inside the tinted doors of the basement level. Reggie and Kelly are putting the finishing touches on the surprise, and I wipe my palms down my thighs. I don't know that I've ever been this nervous. Though I know he can't see me, Reggie's eyes turn in the direction where he knows I'm standing, and that simple gesture calms me. No matter what happens, he is enough to keep me steady.

I'm wearing a simple shift dress with lace trim that cinches slightly at the waist to hug my curves, and my cowboy boots are brand new. My hair is twisted up in a loose bun, and I've pulled out some tendrils to frame my face. I've never been big on taking photos, but I can't wait to have everyone I love together for a memory to last a lifetime. We already have the perfect spot picked out for the frame, and it's somewhere I'll be able to see no matter where we are on the main floor.

"Do you know what I had to do to get away from Taylor?"

I smile and turn to see my pa standing at the bottom of the stairs. He's wearing dark-wash jeans and a white, button-down shirt. He, too, has on cowboy boots, and the love in his eyes nearly takes my breath away.

"You look beautiful," he says, walking up to take my hands. "Your..."

I hold up a hand to keep him from finishing that sentence. Whatever he was going to say is something that I know will make me cry, and the fact his eyes are already wet is making it hard enough to hold myself together. He nods in understanding.

"Are you ready to do this, JoJo?"

"I've never been more ready, Pa."

He opens the sliding glass door, and I walk outside to where

Reggie stands beneath an arbor draped in white. Kelly stands there with him, her smile brighter than I've ever seen it. From the corner of my eye, I catch the photographer moving closer, but I can't pay them any attention because the man I love is holding out his hands for me with tears in his eyes. No sooner do I reach him and take his hands than we turn to look up at the balcony where our families stand with their backs toward us.

"Wait, where's Garrett?" I hear Taylor say.

"I thought Joanna and Reggie were gonna be in these pictures too," Jordan adds.

They look past each other, trying to see in the house when I yell up to them. "We're down here."

Dozens of eyes turn toward us at once, everyone trying to find a spot along the balcony wall to look down at where Reggie and I stand hand-in-hand with Pa off to the side. I hear the shutter of the camera clicking as the photographer catches the photo I've been dreaming about. The surprised and elated faces taking it all in as we turn to face Kelly, and she pronounces us husband and wife in the same spot Reggie found me looking out over the ranch exactly two years ago. It took a lot of try to get here, but this is exactly where I belong.

LEYA LAYNE

Leya Layne's love of a Happily Ever After started with Disney. Then she found romance novels in her early teens thanks to a bag of Harlequin novels hidden under her grandmother's dresser. She got her HEA fix for the rest of her teen years thanks to a well-worn library card. Though she is currently publishing contemporary romances that have been described as Hot Hallmark, don't be surprised to see her delve into historical or paranormal in the future. The possibilities are endless, but the one thing she'll promise is that they'll all be spicy!

Follow Leya all over social media:
https://linktr.ee/LeyaLayneAuthor

See her website for forthcoming releases and trigger/content warnings:
https://bisabelwrites.com/leyas-content-is-for-18-only/

www.ingramcontent.com/pod-product-compliance
Lightning Source LLC
Chambersburg PA
CBHW020035310726
48970CB00007B/2267